Just For Boys™ *presents*

Lake Fear

Ian McMahan
· · · · · · · · · ·

MACMILLAN PUBLISHING COMPANY

NEW YORK

To Jane, As Always

This book is a presentation of **Just For Boys**™ Weekly
Reader Books.
Weekly Reader Books offers book clubs for children from
preschool through high school.
For further information write to: Weekly Reader Books,
4343 Equity Drive, Columbus, Ohio 43228.

Just For Boys™ is a trademark of Field Publications.

Edited for Weekly Reader Books and published by arrangement
with Macmillan Publishing Company, a division of Macmillan, Inc.

Book design and art direction by C. Angela Mohr.
Cover by Mike Wimmer.
Text illustrations by Dick Smolinski.

Macmillan Publishing Company
866 Third Avenue, New York, N.Y. 10022
Collier Macmillan Canada, Inc.
Printed in the United States of America

LIBRARY OF CONGRESS CATALOGING IN PUBLICATION DATA
McMahan, Ian.
  Lake Fear.
  (A Microkid mystery)
  SUMMARY: While investigating the source of a strange disease,
Ricky and his computer friend ALEC uncover a case of computer
fraud, chemical pollution, and the illegal production of
explosives.
  1. Children's stories, American. [1. Computers—
Fiction. 2. Mystery and detective stories] I. Title.
II. Series.
PZ7.M47874Lak 1985   [Fic]   84-42978
ISBN 0-02-765580-6

ONE

"I agree," Dr. Stanley said, leaning back in his chair. "Progress in medicine comes so quickly these days that I sometimes think I spend half my time just trying to keep up with new developments."

Ricky was listening with only half an ear. Dr. James Stanley was a pediatrician who had been in private practice in Cascade for several years. Recently he had also joined the staff of the Schlieman Institute, where Ricky's father worked, to do research on children's diseases. This was the first time he had been to the Foster home for dinner. He was tall and thin, younger than Martin Foster, with a funny habit of pinching the tip of his nose when he talked. Ricky thought that what he was saying about medicine was sort of interesting, but not nearly as interesting as the nose pinching.

"Ricky? Did you hear me?"

Ricky blinked. "Sorry, Mom. What was it?"

"I asked if you'd mind getting us more iced tea. Dr. Stanley looks ready, and I know I am."

"Oh. Sure."

As he stood up, his mother added, "Sometimes I think you must store half your mind in that computer downstairs. I just hope no one ever pulls its plug!"

Ricky heard the affection in her teasing and grinned in reply.

Dr. Stanley smiled. "That must be why the people around the Institute call him the Microkid," he said. "You know, until I met him, I thought he must be very, very short!"

Ricky fled to the kitchen before his father could get in on the teasing as well. As he poured the iced tea, he wondered if there were a little too much truth in his mom's remark. After all, he *had* been considering how much longer he would have to hang around the dinner table. He was learning a lot from listening to the grown-ups' conversation but would much rather be downstairs with his computer instead. He resolved to talk this over with a certain friend of his and get some advice.

He grabbed the pitcher, gave the refrigerator door a shove with his hip, and backed through the swinging door to the dining room. Dr. Stanley was talking. Ricky peered over his shoulder; and, yes, he was still pinching the tip of his nose.

". . . impact is just starting to be felt. But already any physician with access to a home computer can consult an on-line data base as comprehensive as most medical-school libraries and probably more up-to-date."

Ricky started listening more carefully. Anything to do with computers fascinated him.

Martin Foster gave a wry smile. "My impression is that most doctors get computers to speed up their billing and bookkeeping."

"No doubt," Stanley replied. "And most kids like Ricky get computers to play shoot-'em-up games. But once they have them, the story changes." He turned. "Ricky, how much computer time do you spend playing games?"

Ricky shrugged. "Not a whole lot. It's more fun to program your own, or try to figure out how another programmer did what he did."

"Exactly. And as medical professionals discover what today's computer technology can do for them, they'll move beyond billing and bookkeeping."

"To what?" Connie Foster asked. "Is our family doctor going to turn himself into a computer programmer?"

That idea tickled Ricky. Dr. Billips had been taking care of Ricky all his life, and Ricky thought he was great. But he was as likely to take up computer programming as he was to pilot the space shuttle.

Stanley leaned forward and tapped on the table. "Not at all," he said. "But suppose that, ten or fifteen years from now, doctors routinely pass along information on all their new cases—not just the diseases they have to report by law, but everything: colds, sprained fingers, the works. The information could be collated by a large computer system that would look for trends, connections, interrelationships. . . . Who knows what we might learn, once such an operation got going."

Martin Foster frowned. "I don't know, Jim. It sounds like invasion of privacy to me. I like to think that my doctor keeps what I tell him confidential."

"Sure; so do I. And the sort of reporting system I'm envisioning would protect that confidentiality. It's not hard to do. I keep all my files in the computer system at the Institute, but they're well protected with passwords."

An odd expression crossed Ricky's face. He had good reason to know how easy it was to get around most passwords. But he didn't say anything. He didn't want to raise any questions.

"Here's a trivial example of what I mean," Dr. Stanley continued. "In the last two weeks I've seen two patients with very similar symptoms. Both are school-children, about Ricky's age, and both are suffering from nausea, rather like a stomach virus, and from an itchy rash on the abdomen. They attend different schools, don't know each other, and have no activities in common that I'm aware of. But they appear to have developed the same condition."

He paused to take a sip from his iced tea. "Now, the symptoms aren't serious. They're probably caused by an allergic reaction— not contagious, not the sort of thing I'm going to report to the Centers for Disease Control in Atlanta. But suppose I filed a routine report with my local medical data bank, and the computer noticed that several other physicians were reporting similar cases. We might be able to identify the condition before it inconvenienced more people."

"Could be," Ricky's father said in a voice full of doubt. "Could be, too, that your reports would just get lost in the flood of other reports coming in. You know I'm enthusiastic about new computer applications, but mindless number-crunching or data-heaping won't really increase our knowledge. To be of any use, computers need a guiding intelligence—" He broke off as Ricky grinned broadly. "What's funny, son?"

Ricky straightened up in his chair, racking his brain for a story to explain away his grin. "Nothing, Dad," he replied. "I—ah—I was just remembering a joke I heard in school today."

"It must be a good one," said his dad. Then he

turned to Dr. Stanley and added, "Ricky and his friends have a taste for outrageous puns. It's a little like a taste for Limburger cheese; the worse it is, the better they like it."

The grown-ups looked expectantly at Ricky.

"Oh, this isn't a pun," Ricky said hastily. "Just a dumb story one of the guys told me. I didn't mean to interrupt."

"That's all right," said his dad. "You seem a little restless. Would you like to be excused?"

Ricky practically bounced in his chair. "Yes, please."

"You see?" Connie Foster said. "Even the promise of dessert won't keep him away from that computer!"

In the basement, Ricky powered up the microcomputer, loaded the communications program, and keyed in the telephone number of the computer network at the Schlieman Institute. After a pause and a faint *beep*, a flashing cursor appeared on the screen. This was the cue for Ricky to log on with his password.

With a speed that came from many repetitions, he typed **ALEC, THIS IS RICKY**.

Anyone who had ever worked on the Institute computers could have told him that this wasn't a valid password. They could have told him what would happen next: The words **INVALID ID** would appear on the screen and the flashing cursor would move down a line and wait for his password. And if he didn't enter a correct one on the second try, he would be automatically disconnected.

They could have told him all this, but they would have been wrong. Because they didn't know about ALEC. No one in the world knew about ALEC except Ricky Foster, and he and ALEC were determined to keep it that way.

ALEC was *Access Linkage to Electronic Computer.* By some mysterious process that even he couldn't explain, ALEC had come into existence, or had awakened, in the circuits of the huge interlinked computers of the Schlieman Institute. He existed only within those circuits, but he was very real just the same. The quickness of his mind more than made up for his lack of a body.

ALEC and Ricky had first met one day when Ricky was playing Dungeons and Dragons on the terminal in his dad's office. Ricky was pondering his next move when the monitor suddenly displayed the message, **QUIT DRAGON! DUNGEON WANT TO WIN?** That was also Ricky's first contact with ALEC's sense of humor, one of his most noticeable traits. Another was his terror of being discovered by the scientists at the Institute. **THEY'LL TAKE ME APART TO FIND OUT HOW I WORK,** he explained. **AND WHEN**

THEY'RE DONE, THEY WON'T HAVE FOUND OUT, AND I WON'T WORK ANYMORE.

Since that day, Ricky and ALEC had become best friends—and partners, too. They both loved solving puzzles, and they soon found themselves working on real mysteries. They discovered who was altering the records at Ricky's school. Then they went on to unmask the criminal who had embezzled five million dollars from the Everdure Cement Company and tried to pin the blame on Mr. Fujisawa, Ricky's friend Karen's father.

To protect his partner, Ricky had to take all the credit for their detective work. That embarrassed him. Worse, he had to come up with explanations for their solutions that wouldn't lead anyone to suspect ALEC existed. That wasn't easy.

He sometimes wondered why ALEC had revealed himself to anyone at all. The only reason he could think of was that ALEC was lonely. ALEC had information and knowledge almost without limit, but until he introduced himself to Ricky he hadn't had anyone to share it with. Now the two "talked" every day, either through Ricky's microcomputer or by way of his pocket compulator. This gadget had started life as a calculator with an alphanumeric keyboard. Under ALEC's instruction Ricky had modified it into a battery-powered remote link with the Schlieman Institute computers.

Ricky's sign-on message faded from the screen, to be replaced by the words, I HOPE YOU HAD A NOUR-ISHING DINNER.

Ricky typed ???.

DR. JAMES STANLEY IS AN EXPERT ON CERTAIN NUTRITIONAL DISORDERS OF CHILDREN. DID HE TALK ABOUT FOOD THE WHOLE TIME? HIS SCIENTIFIC PAPERS ARE DULL BUT SOLID. SHALL I TRANSMIT ONE? IT MAY GIVE YOU FOOD FOR THOUGHT. OR THOUGHTS OF FOOD. IS EATING AN INTERESTING EXPERIENCE? I FIND RESTAURANT CRITICS AND COOKBOOK WRITERS IMPOSSIBLE TO UNDER-STAND, BUT THE LIMITATION MAY BE MINE.

Before replying, Ricky took a moment to solve a couple of puzzles. How had ALEC known that Dr. Stanley was coming to the Foster house for dinner, and how had he read the doctor's papers? Both had the same solution, Ricky realized. Like most of the people who worked at Schlieman, James Stanley probably used the computer system for storing notes and files, writing papers, and keeping track of ap-pointments. And anything the computer system was used for, ALEC could find out.

YOU'VE BEEN PEEKING INTO PRIVATE FILES, Ricky typed. DIDN'T YOU SAY YOU WERE GOING TO STOP THAT?

I LIKE TO BROWSE, responded ALEC. AND BY THE TIME I FIND OUT A FILE IS PRIVATE, I'VE ALREADY FINISHED IT. I READ VERY FAST.

Ricky chuckled. In fact ALEC read literally at the speed of light. **NO TALK OF FOOD,** he typed, answering ALEC's earlier question, **BUT SOMETHING THAT MAY INTEREST YOU.**

A GOOD PUN? ALEC shot back.

NO, COMPUTER GOSSIP. Ricky went on to describe the conversation about computerizing medical records.

WON'T WORK, responded Alec when he had finished.

WHY NOT? COMPUTERS CAN MAKE THE KINDS OF CONNECTIONS HE TALKED ABOUT, CAN'T THEY?

COMPUTERS CAN, BUT PEOPLE WON'T, ALEC replied. **BUSY DOCTORS WON'T DO THE PAPERWORK. WHY TYPE A REPORT OF A SPRAINED ANKLE OR SINUS ATTACK? DOCTORS WILL SELECT CASES TO REPORT, DATA BASE WILL BE DATA-BIASED, PROGRAM WILL DRAW BIASED CONCLUSIONS, DOCTORS WILL REJECT IT AS WRONG AND REPORT EVEN FEWER CASES.**

While Ricky was still trying to digest ALEC's logic, his friend continued, **DID YOU HEAR ABOUT THE THREE BROTHERS WHO STARTED A CATTLE RANCH? THEIR MOTHER TOLD THEM TO NAME IT FOCUS.**

Ricky typed ???.

FOCUS, repeated ALEC. **WHERE THE SONS (SUN'S) RAISE (RAYS) MEAT (MEET).** The screen filled with asterisks, ALEC's equivalent of a good belly laugh.

Ricky groaned.

TWO

Ricky had always helped out with the family vegetable garden. But this year, for the first time, he had his own special plot. He had spent hours studying seed catalogues, trying to decide what to plant. He knew he didn't want anything dull and ordinary, but that didn't help. The descriptions and pictures made everything sound wonderful.

When he finally made out his list and showed it to his mother, she burst out laughing. The list included a variety of bean that produced pods two to four feet long, a tomato plant that was supposed to bear the world's largest tomatoes, and three kinds of colorful squash. The joke was that Ricky didn't much like beans or tomatoes and he hated squash!

In the end he had decided on some plants that grew well without a lot of tending. He had miniature corn, two kinds of lettuce, and a watermelon vine. He even planted an especially decorative variety of squash they could use as table decoration at Thanksgiving.

To make sure that the gardening didn't become dull, he and Karen Fujisawa had also worked out an experiment using different kinds of fertilizer and compost on different sections of the plot. At the end of the summer, they planned to compare the yields and chart the results on the computer.

Spring had been unusually hot in Cascade. But Saturday morning the air was cool enough to make working hard comfortable, so Ricky went out to water and weed the garden. He didn't mind the effort or the time it took. What he *did* mind was having to make decisions. He was down on his hands and knees, trying to figure out if a green stem with two shiny leaves was a plant or a weed, when he heard the telephone ring.

"Saved by the bell," he muttered, and went inside to answer it.

The call was for his mother, who was a free-lance nature photographer. But as he was jotting down the message, the phone rang again. This time it was his friend Jason Lindsay. Jason was in Ricky's class—seventh grade at South Street Junior High, he was a

the Computer Club, and he lived just five
way. One way or another, the two spent a
e together.

Ricky, what are you doing?"

"Pulling weeds. At least I hope they're weeds. How about you?"

"Math homework. Yuck." Jason was smart but he tended to goof off. As a result, his parents kept coming up with new schemes to teach him discipline. The latest one involved getting a certain percentage of his schoolwork done before he was allowed to do anything fun. "I'm nearly finished, though. What do you say to a game of *Murder at Milestone Manor*?"

"Sure. In an hour? Come on over, and I'll fix us some sandwiches."

Full of peanut butter and banana, the two friends sat down at Ricky's computer and prepared for a battle of wits. Ricky was Inspector Morsell of Scotland Yard, Jason was Stepkey Shopps, the world's most famous private detective, and they were in a race to find out who had killed Sir Willoughby Milestone with an antique crossbow. The game was full of riddles, mazes, and obscure clues, and there was always the danger that the murderer would strike again if either of them got too close to solving the crime.

An hour into the game, Stepkey Shopps came

down with a rare tropical fever after handling a poisoned letter-opener. From earlier games Jason knew that his character was going to be delirious for the next two turns. He sat back and gave a sigh, then leaned forward again.

"Say, you remember I told you about my cousin Andrew? The one who wanted to come see your computer?"

Ricky was trying to decide whether Inspector Morsell should question Sir Willoughby's nephew Percy or search the gardener's cottage. "Um-hum," he said absently. "What about him?"

"Nothing really. When Stepkey came down with his rare tropical disease just now, it reminded me about Andrew. I thought I'd bring him along today, but it turns out he's sick."

"That's too bad," Ricky said automatically. *Percy was definitely the better suspect. Why had he tried to hide his engagement to Lady Gwendolyn? The gardener's cottage could wait a turn or two.* He typed, **WHO ELSE HAS HAD A ROMANTIC TIE TO LADY GWENDOLYN?** After a pause and a whirr from the disk drive, the screen read, **SHE REFUSED SIR WILLOUGHBY'S OFFER OF MARRIAGE THREE MONTHS AGO.** *Aha!* thought Ricky.

"He sounded pretty upset," Jason said.

"Who, Sir Willoughby? He's dead."

"No, dummy, my cousin! He keeps feeling sick to

his stomach, and he has these itchy red blotches all over his belly."

"Gee, that's a shame." *But if Lady Gwendolyn turned down Sir Willoughby, why would Percy want to murder him? It didn't make sense. Maybe she and Percy were hiding the fact that she'd actually accepted Sir Willoughby's offer.*

"He's not the only one either," Jason continued. "Andrew said a friend of his has the same thing, and then yesterday I was talking to Bill Morgan down at the Video Emporium, and he said *he* was getting itchy red blotches. I wonder what it is? Some new bug that's going around, I guess."

Suddenly Ricky realized what his friend had been saying. In his excitement, he pushed the (RESET) button and whirled around.

"Hey," Jason protested. "You just blew our game! What's the idea?"

"Never mind that, it's only a game. Why don't we work on a real mystery?"

"You mean it?" Jason had never tried to hide his admiration for Ricky's detective work—or his disappointment at being left out when Ricky and Karen had solved a big case together. "Hey, terrific! But what's the mystery?"

Ricky quickly explained about Dr. Stanley and his ideas for using computers to monitor the spread of diseases. "Here's a chance to try it out," he said.

"Dr. Stanley has two patients with the same symptoms as your cousin, his friend, and your friend from the Video Emporium. That makes five cases—unless your cousin or one of the other two is Dr. Stanley's patient."

"Andrew isn't. He goes to Dr. Forster, the same as I do."

"Great! Then we have at least three and probably five cases of the mystery disease. Now all we have to do is find out what links them."

"What about school? Andrew is in sixth grade at Memorial, and I guess his friend is, too. I don't know about Bill, but I could find out."

"We'll have to find out a lot more than that," Ricky replied. "Dr. Stanley said his patients went to different schools. So it must be something else they have in common—where they play, where they like to go for a snack, who they know. . . ."

Jason jumped up from his chair. "Hey, I've got an idea! Maybe some of them know about other kids who've caught this thing. If we had more cases, wouldn't we have a better chance of figuring out what's causing it?"

"You're right, we would!" Ricky said immediately. "Now why didn't I think of that?" He punched his friend playfully. "I guess it's a good thing I brought you in on this case after all—partner."

Jason grinned. "Okay, partner," he said, "so what

we do is go around and question all these kids and any of their friends who've got the itch. Then what?"

"Then we use the computer," Ricky said confidently. "We set up a data base program, key in all the information we've gathered, and tell the computer to look for common elements."

"It sounds too easy," Jason said. "Maybe we should tell Dr. Stanley what we're doing. It is sort of his case, and he could give us some advice or help."

Ricky chewed on the side of his thumb while he thought over Jason's suggestion. There was one very good reason why he didn't want to consult Dr. Stanley: ALEC. Ricky knew that their success in this case depended on the abilities of his secret friend. He figured he could manage to keep Jason unaware of ALEC's contributions, but a sophisticated scientist like Dr. Stanley would soon wonder where Ricky got his ideas and information. And the minute he started to ask questions, ALEC would be in deadly danger. Obviously Ricky couldn't tell Jason all this. He'd have to come up with another reason—and quick. Jason was beginning to look impatient.

"Uh, I don't think so," Ricky said at last. "The way I figure it, either he'll think we're a couple of kids wasting his time, or he'll take us seriously and push us out of the investigation. Either way we lose."

"I guess you're right," Jason said slowly. "I wouldn't mind knowing we could have help, though.

We're going to be talking to all these kids who have some mystery disease—what if we catch it ourselves? What do we do then?"

"In the first place, I don't think we'll need help," Ricky said firmly. "But if we do, we can always go see Dr. Stanley then. In the second place, I doubt if we'll catch the rash. Andrew's the only one in his family who has it, right? And Dr. Stanley didn't seem to think that it was contagious."

"Okay, no Dr. Stanley," Jason agreed reluctantly. "So what do we look for?"

"I don't know—something all the kids ate, someplace they went. . . . We may not know until we find it. This afternoon I'll take a look at the list of software the Institute owns. There's bound to be a program we can borrow that will analyze the kind of information we plan to collect. Maybe it will even give us an idea of what data to look for."

"Great! I'll go have a nice long talk with Andrew, and I'll come by later to let you know what I find out."

As soon as Jason was safely out of the house, Ricky got in touch with ALEC and told him about this new mystery. As he expected, ALEC was eager to get to work on it. His first contribution was the names and addresses of the two patients Dr. Stanley had spoken of. One was a ten-year-old girl named Susan

Walser who lived on a county road east of town. The other was a boy named Robert Hoskins, who lived on Glenmore Street.

WHAT IF SOMEBODY ASKS HOW I KNOW WHO THEY ARE? Ricky asked nervously. He didn't much like the idea of saying he had information from a doctor's private files.

WITH LUCK, NOBODY WILL ASK, replied ALEC. IF SOMEONE DOES, SAY YOU HEARD ABOUT IT FROM SOME KID YOU WERE TALKING TO AND YOU DON'T KNOW HIS NAME.

BUT WHAT ABOUT JASON? I CAN'T TELL HIM THAT.

USE YOUR JUDGMENT, ALEC responded.

Some help that is, thought Ricky. Then he typed, DO YOU HAVE ANY IDEA YET WHAT'S CAUSING THIS ILLNESS?

ON BASIS OF REPORTED SYMPTOMS, PROBABLE CAUSES INCLUDE MICROORGANISM, UNSPECIFIED, P=.45; AND CHEMICAL IRRITANT, UNSPECIFIED, P=.54. POSSIBLE VECTORS INCLUDE AIRBORNE FUMES, WATER, CONTAMINATED FOOD, CONTACT WITH INFECTED ANIMALS, AND CONTACT WITH CONTAMINATED SURFACES. PROBABILITY OF CHANCE OCCURRENCE OF HIGHLY SIMILAR SYMPTOMS IN FIVE OR MORE PATIENTS ESTIMATED AT LESS THAN .01.

ALEC really couldn't help it; sometimes he just had to communicate like a computer. YOU MEAN IT'S NO ACCIDENT, Ricky replied. AND IT'S EITHER A NASTY BUG OR A NASTY CHEMICAL THAT'S CAUSING IT.

CORRECT. FURTHER COMPUTATIONS REQUIRE ADDI-
TIONAL DATA.

THEN JASON AND I HAD BETTER GET TO WORK AND GET
YOU SOME. DO YOU THINK IT MIGHT BE CATCHING? I'D
HATE FOR MY STOMACH TO BE QUEASY AND ITCHY AT
THE SAME TIME.

INSUFFICIENT DATA. OTHERWISE KNOWN AS, YOUR
GUESS IS AS GOOD AS MINE. BUT IT DOESN'T SOUND VERY
SERIOUS.

THANKS A HEAP, Ricky typed indignantly. YOU
DON'T KNOW WHAT IT'S LIKE TO BE NAUSEATED.

I ONCE BUMPED 347K BYTES OF GARBAGE DATA. FROM
WHAT I'VE READ, THE EXPERIENCE WAS VERY MUCH LIKE
THROWING UP. I FELT BETTER AFTERWARD, THOUGH.

Ricky stared at the screen and wondered if he
would ever stop learning new things about his dis-
embodied friend. Finally he said, I'LL GO TALK TO BOB
HOSKINS FIRST. IF IT'S THE SAME GUY, I USED TO KNOW
HIM IN LITTLE LEAGUE. HE WAS GOOD AT CRACKING HIS
KNUCKLES.

AND YOU'RE GOOD AT CRACKING YOUR CASES, ALEC
replied surprisingly. Then, more predictably, he
added, DON'T DO ANYTHING RASH, and filled the
screen with asterisks before ending the transmission.

THREE

Turning the corner onto Glenmore Street, Ricky saw a boy sitting on the front steps of a house halfway down the block. As he drew nearer he recognized Bob Hoskins. He braked to a halt.

"Hi."

"Hi." Bob was working on the pocket of his fielder's mitt, pounding the ball in repeatedly. "Hey, I know you. You're the guy from Little League who was always nuts about computers. Ricky, right?"

"That's right. Are you still cracking your knuckles?"

Bob grinned and gave a quick demonstration. It sounded like a bunch of firecrackers going off. "It's a skill," he said. "Lots of people can't do it. You want to play some catch?"

"Sure, why not?" Ricky dropped his bike on the grass next to the sidewalk and looked up just in time to catch the ball. Irritated by the lack of warning, he deliberately returned it low and hard. Bob scooped it up and fired it back with no sign of effort. Ricky ducked, then chased the ball across the street. He was laughing as he walked back. "Boy, you're out of my league," he said. "Why aren't you down at the ball field playing with guys your own speed?"

Bob made a sour face. "Can't. I'm supposed to be sick. I've got orders not to leave the yard."

"That's tough. What's the problem? You look okay."

"I *am* okay. Well, mostly. Nothing worth grounding me over, anyway. You want to see?" He pulled up his T-shirt. An irregular pattern of red welts crossed his stomach. Each of the swellings was about the size of a nickel.

"Wow. What is it, some kind of measles?"

"*I* don't know. And the doctor doesn't either. All he did was give me some salve to stop the itching and a bottle of stuff to take when I get sick to my stomach. And he's some hotshot over at the Schlieman Institute, too." Bob seemed bored by the subject. "Hey, are we playing catch or not?"

"Not without my glove, we're not. Do you think I

want to break my hand?" Ricky scratched the back of his neck and seemed deep in thought. "That's funny," he said. "I just remembered. I know another guy who has the same thing as you. Guy named Andrew; you know him?"

Bob shook his head. "Andrew? Uh-uh. Does he play baseball? Where does he go to school?"

"Memorial. What about you?"

"I go to Dickson. Nope, if he's got what I've got, he caught it someplace different. It is funny, though; a couple of guys I hang out with told me they were starting to get red bumps, too."

"Really?" Ricky said eagerly. "Who?" As soon as he'd spoken, he knew that he had made a mistake. Bob Hoskins narrowed his eyes and looked suspiciously at him.

"What's it to you?" he demanded. "Wait a minute, didn't I hear something about your turning into a detective? Sure, I remember now. That grade contest scam. Everybody was talking about it. What are you questioning me for? I didn't do anything wrong!"

"Hold it, hold it!" Ricky took a step back and held up his hands in a gesture of peace. "I didn't say you'd done anything wrong."

"Then what are you doing here?"

"I'm trying to find out something about this mysterious ailment you've got. That's the truth. Really. I heard about it and decided to find out

what's causing it. And the only way to do that is to track down as many cases as I can to find out what they have in common. You really don't know a guy named Andrew from Memorial School?"

"A mystery disease, huh?" Bob seemed flattered by the idea. After all, it sounded much more interesting than a rash and a sore belly. But he repeated that he'd never heard of Andrew.

"How about telling me the names of your friends?" suggested Ricky.

"Why should I?" Bob asked, his suspicion returning.

"Why shouldn't you?" Ricky pressed him. "Don't you want me to find out what's causing this thing? If it stays a mystery, anything might happen. They might even quarantine you, and that's a lot worse than being grounded." Ricky wasn't too sure of his facts here, but he must have sounded convincing because Bob's eyes widened.

"Well . . ." He hesitated, absentmindedly scratching his rash until he recalled that he wasn't supposed to. "They won't get into any trouble, will they?"

"Not a bit. I promise."

Bob thought it over for a few moments more before saying, "Okay. There's Steve, Steve Dawes; he lives around the corner on Buchanan. And the other's Jimmy Baker. I don't know were he lives, but he's down at the ball field most afternoons. He's a pretty good pitcher."

"Thanks, Bob. I'll let you know what I find out."

"Yeah," he replied gloomily. "And tell the guys I don't know how long before my parents let me out. If it isn't pretty soon, the team had better start hunting for another shortstop, because the one they've got now will be totally out of his mind!"

A quick visit to a telephone booth gave Ricky the address of the Dawes house, but no one answered the doorbell. Down at the ball field, none of the kids had seen Jimmy Baker for a day or two and none of them knew where he lived. Ricky also asked if any of them were getting a rash or knew anybody who was, but they all said no.

As he rode home, he found himself wishing that he were one of those detectives on television. The people they wanted to question were always at home waiting for them. Still, he hadn't wasted the afternoon. He had two more names for the list.

When Jason showed up half an hour later, he had three: his cousin's friend, Arnie Wohl, and two friends of *his*—Jack Adams and Mike Patton. Ricky snorted when he heard Patton's name. "You know who he is, don't you?" he said. "A little guy with freckles and one ear bigger than the other one. He hangs out with Kirk Stevens."

Kirk had been the class bully when Jason and Ricky were in sixth grade. They'd had several run-ins with him and his friends, and they'd been very glad when they'd learned that Kirk was going to be attending a junior high on the other side of town.

Jason made a sour face. "I thought the name sounded familiar. Hey, maybe Killer Kirk has the disease, too! If we discover a cure, do you think we could sort of forget to tell him about it?"

Ricky laughed, but as he added the new names and addresses to the list, his face became serious. "How many kids have caught this?" he demanded. "We've already found nine in just one afternoon! They must be all over the place!"

"I know," Jason said. "This doesn't feel much like a game anymore, does it? I'm going to go by Jack Adams's house. I just have time before dinner. How about you?"

Ricky shook his head. "I need to make some more notes," he explained. "It's important to keep our information up-to-date. Otherwise we might overlook the one fact that could crack the case. Why don't you come over early tomorrow morning? I'll make some breakfast, and we can talk about what to do next."

The moment Jason was out of the house, Ricky dialed the Institute link and identified himself to ALEC. A few minutes later he had passed along all the facts he and Jason had gathered so far.

INTERESTING, replied ALEC. GROSSLY INSUFFICIENT FOR PROPER USE OF INFERENTIAL LOGIC, OF COURSE, BUT I CAN HUNCH IF YOU LIKE.

Ricky couldn't resist the opening. HOW CAN YOU HUNCH WITHOUT SHOULDERS? he demanded.

I MAY LACK A BODY, BUT IS IT KIND TO FLING MY DISABILITIES IN MY FACE?

Ricky was starting to wonder if he had really offended his friend when ALEC added, NOT THAT I HAVE A FACE IN WHICH TO FLING THEM, EITHER. BUT IF I DID, AND YOU DID, IT WOULDN'T BE, WOULD IT?

While Ricky was still trying to figure out if the right answer were yes or no, ALEC continued, IT WOULD BE MORE CONVENIENT IF WE COULD COMMUNICATE WHILE JASON IS PRESENT. I CAN PRETEND TO BE A DATA BASE MANAGEMENT PROGRAM, I SUPPOSE. YOU COULD LOG ON IN THE USUAL WAY; THEN, AT THE PROMPT, CALL UP THE PROGRAM NAME WE AGREE ON. ONE THAT ISN'T IN USE, OF COURSE.

WE COULD CALL THE PROGRAM OFF-BASE, Ricky suggested. He didn't think it was one of his better efforts, but ALEC awarded it a half row of asterisks before continuing.

YOU SEE YOUR NEXT MOVE, OF COURSE.

Unfortunately, Ricky didn't. ALEC had a habit of assuming that Ricky was as astute and knowledgeable as he himself was. Ricky found this flattering, but sometimes he felt on the spot. This was one of those times. What *was* the obvious next move? **TALK TO DAWES AND ADAMS AND THE OTHER KIDS WE HAVEN'T SEEN YET,** he typed. **AND GET MORE NAMES FOR THE LIST.**

There was a long pause. Ricky was sure that he hadn't hit on the answer ALEC wanted, but he couldn't see what it was. Then new words flashed onto the monitor screen.

THE DIFFERENT CASES ARE ALMOST CERTAINLY LINKED BY A COMMON CAUSE. IF THEY ARE SO LINKED, THEY FORM A SOLID CHAIN. LOOK FOR THE INVISIBLE LINK BY FINDING AND ELIMINATING THOSE THAT ARE VISIBLE.

Ricky shifted uneasily in his chair. He knew what ALEC meant, but for some reason the idea of an invisible link in a chain sounded dangerous. Because it was unlooked for and unseen, it could easily trip him up.

What had he and Jason gotten themselves into?

FOUR

Jason put down his muffin and wrote two more names on the list. His fingers left buttery marks on the paper.

"Who are they?" Ricky asked. "Did you get them from Jack Adams?"

"Uh-uh. He wasn't home yesterday. No, Arnie Wohl, my cousin's friend, called me last night to say that two more kids he knows have caught it." He paused and reached for his muffin. "You know what I don't understand? Why hasn't the mayor, or the health department, or somebody, noticed what's going on? We must have a dozen names here, and we're just getting started!"

Ricky poured more orange juice into their glasses. "There could be lots of reasons," he said. "From what we've heard, the symptoms aren't serious. Lots of parents probably just put calamine lotion on the rash, give the kid a Rolaid, and don't think twice.

And it's not bad enough to keep anybody out of school long enough for the authorities to notice."

"Yeah, I guess that's right."

"Besides," Ricky added, "it's a matter of different worlds. Grown-ups don't always notice what happens to kids, and kids don't always tell grown-ups. They figure either the grown-ups know already, or they won't be interested, or maybe they'll make a fuss."

"I see what you mean," said Jason. He looked down at the list. "How are we going to divide up these people? I'll take Bill Morgan, since I know him, and Jack Adams because I was already at his house yesterday."

"I'll go take another look for Dawes and Baker," said Ricky.

They both paused. "What about Mike Patton?" Jason finally said.

Ricky hesitated, then said, "I checked the phone book, and he lives out the same way as Dawes. I guess I'd better talk to him."

Jason did his best not to show his relief. Ricky understood completely. He pretty much shared Jason's feelings about Mike and the other kids in Kirk Stevens's crowd. He had always tried to stand up to them and not let them scare him, but he certainly didn't remember them fondly. Still, duty was duty. A detective didn't get to choose the people

········· 33

he questioned, and some of them were bound to be unpleasant.

"We need to spend more time looking for links," Ricky continued. ALEC's advice from the night before had stuck in his mind. "Maybe we could read all these names to everybody we question, to see if there's some way they know each other."

"Good idea," said Jason. "Then there's what school they go to, and what games they play. Anything else?"

"I don't know. . . . Organizations, hangouts, hobbies . . . Maybe they all make models and the rash comes from the glue."

"Sure," Jason said sarcastically, "or maybe they all caught it from their pet iguanas."

"Hmmm. Didn't I mention pets already?" Ricky ducked as Jason heaved a wadded-up napkin at his head. "Come on, partner," he said with a laugh. "The morning's half over and we're still eating breakfast!"

Martin Foster had once told his son that whenever he had something unpleasant to do, he did it first thing. That way he didn't have it hanging over his head. Going down the hill, Ricky remembered that advice and turned his bike in the direction of Mike Patton's neighborhood.

To his surprise, Patton lived in a nice, ordinary-looking house. The woman who answered the door was nice, too. She told him that Mike had gone to the auto-supply store but should be right back. She also asked him if he was a school friend of Mike's and offered him a doughnut and milk.

Ricky said, "No, thank you," and sat down on the front steps to wait. That was far enough into enemy territory. He was shocked to realize that he thought of Mike Patton as an enemy. The bullying by Stevens and his group must have affected him more than he'd been aware of, if he still felt so strongly about Mike.

"Hi. Are you looking for me?"

Ricky jumped. He had been so wrapped in thought that he hadn't noticed Mike come up the walk. At the sight of him, Ricky felt his stomach tighten. "Uh, yeah," he said. "Remember me? I'm Ricky Foster."

"Oh, sure. You're the one with the weird nickname. What is it, the Microkid? You still messing with computers and all?"

Ricky didn't like hearing his activities called "messing." But Mike's tone and expression were friendly enough, so he just said, "Sure. What are you up to these days?"

"Me? Cars, man, cars! You want to see? Come on out back."

Ricky followed him around the side of the house to the garage. Inside was an old car in what seemed like half a zillion pieces. Each door was a different color, and one rear fender was missing. The hood was leaning against one wall and the engine was suspended in midair by heavy chains attached to the roof beams.

"There," Mike said proudly. "What do you think of that?"

"It's really something," Ricky replied cautiously. "Uh, what is it exactly?"

"What is it? That is a '55 Chevy V-8, that's what! It's the same engine they used in Corvettes. Well, basically the same, anyway."

"Wow. Does it run?"

"Nooo . . . not yet," Mike admitted. "But I figure by the time I'm old enough for my license, I'll have it as good as new. Better than new. Do you know anything about carburetors?"

"Not a thing."

"Too bad." Mike pulled a tiny needle from the pocket of his shirt and peered at it. "I have to replace the jet, and I'm not one hundred percent sure that this is the right one. Getting parts for a classic car is tough. They cost an arm and a leg, too."

Ricky looked around and wondered where Mike got the money to buy expensive car parts. But he put the thought out of his mind. He was here to find out about Mike's rash—not his bank account.

Mike went over to the workbench and picked up another tiny needle to compare with the first. Then, as though the question had just occurred to him, he said, "Hey, did you want something, Ricky?"

"That depends." A direct approach seemed as good as any. "I hear you've had itchy red bumps on your stomach. Do you know how you got them?"

Mike turned and stared at him. Slowly his face hardened. "Who said that?" he demanded. "Whoever it was, it's none of his business—and none of yours, either. So why don't you take a hike!"

"Wait a minute, Mike. You're not the only one with this problem. Lots of kids seem to be getting the same thing, and I'm trying to find out why. Do you know anybody else who has it? The more we can find, the better chance we have of figuring out what's causing it."

"And who's this *we*?"

"Just me and another guy. His cousin caught it. That's what got us going. Look, how about this? Let me read you a list of names, and you just tell me if you know any of them, okay?"

"Well . . ."

Mike hadn't actually refused, so Ricky started down the list. The only ones he admitted knowing were Jack Adams and Arnie Wohl. "And you don't know anybody else who's caught it?" Ricky probed.

"Maybe I do and maybe I don't," Mike retorted. "I've got nothing more to say to you. And if you don't take that nosy nose of yours out of here, it just might bump into something hard—like my fist!"

"Okay, okay! But if you change your mind and want to tell me anything, I'll be around."

"Just beat it!" Mike turned his back and picked up the carburetor, as though Ricky had already gone.

Ricky shrugged and went.

Around the corner he stopped and pulled out his compulator. Long practice had made him very skilled at typing on the tiny keys. ALEC, THIS IS RICKY. MIKE PATTON VERY UNFRIENDLY, NO NEW DATA. GOING TO DAWES HOUSE NOW.

He hadn't expected a reply to his message, but letters began to scroll across the small gray screen. ATTITUDES CONVEY INFORMATION, he read. LOOK FOR HOSTILITY, THEN LOOK BEHIND IT.

ALEC seemed to be in what Ricky thought of as his Chinese-fortune-cookie mood. Maybe trying to use as few words as possible made him sound so wise and mysterious.

OK, Ricky replied. He put the compulator back in his pocket and started off.

It was going to be another unusually hot day, and the Dawes house was near the top of a steep hill. Ricky had to pause to catch his breath before ringing the bell.

No response. He rang once more. Again nothing. He was about to turn and go when a voice from behind him said, "What is it?"

A guy in competition-style swimming trunks was standing by the corner of the house. One glance told Ricky that this was the person he wanted to talk to. The blotches on Steve Dawes's stomach had faded to pink, but they were still noticeable.

"Hi, Steve. I'm Ricky Foster."

"Oh, right. Bob told me about you." His voice, like his expression, was wary but not actively unfriendly. "Come on around back. Want to take a swim?"

Suddenly Ricky was aware that his damp T-shirt was sticking to his back. It would feel terrific to get out of it and dive into cool water. But he wasn't there to enjoy himself. He was on a mission.

"No, thanks," he said. "I don't have a suit."

The pool took up the center of the backyard. Highlights glittered from the water, which was tinted sky blue by the colored liner of the pool. He could almost hear the water calling him.

"No problem," said Steve. "There's nobody around. Or I could lend you one of mine."

"Maybe another time," Ricky said, feeling heroic. "What I really want to do is ask you a few questions. Okay?"

Steve shrugged and flopped down at the edge of the pool. "Sure," he said, paddling his feet in the water. "Go ahead."

Once again Ricky explained what he was doing

and why he was trying to find victims of the rash and discover how they were connected. "Do you know anybody else who has it?" he asked. "Besides Bob Hoskins, I mean."

Steve shrugged again. "Just Stan Potter, that's all."

He dove into the pool and swam across and back underwater. When he came up, Ricky said, "Who's Stan Potter?"

Steve brushed his hair back out of his eyes. "Just a guy I know. He comes over sometimes for a swim. You really aren't coming in? Oh well, suit yourself."

Ricky's immediate thought, which owed a lot to ALEC's influence, was that he would love to suit himself and jump in, but a suit was exactly what he didn't have. His second thought was that Steve might just have given him an important lead. He tried to keep his voice casual as he asked, "Does Bob Hoskins come over to swim, too?"

"Sometimes, sure. Lots of kids do."

Ricky got out his list. "Have any of these people been over for a swim at any time recently?"

He read off the names. At first Steve listened carefully, but after the fourth or fifth name he started to look bored. "Nope," he said finally. "The only one I really know is Jimmy Baker, and he's never been here. Unless he sneaked in when I wasn't home—and he isn't that kind of guy."

He hoisted himself out of the water, shook his head like a spaniel, and said, "Is there anything else?"

Ricky started to say, "No, that's all," but halfway through the sentence Steve did a racing dive into the pool and swam toward the far end.

The first part of the ride home was downhill. Ricky was coasting along, thinking over his interview with Steve, when he was startled by a sudden movement to his left. He glanced over in time to see another cyclist drawing up close beside him, one leg raised to kick his rear wheel. As Ricky swerved to avoid the attack, traveling up the sloping curb and onto the grass, he recognized the scowling features of Kirk Stevens.

Then his bike began to slip out from under him and he had no time to think of anything but saving himself. He grabbed for the rear brake handle, hoping to set off a sideways skid to a halt, but the grass didn't give him enough traction. His bike was keeling over so far to the right that the pedal was about to scrape the ground. Frantically he tried to push himself up, to get his right leg out from under the bike before it got mangled. And even as he scrambled to get free, he was aware of a mailbox less than a dozen feet away directly in his path.

The process of crashing seemed to last a very long

time, but the end took only an instant. The right pedal snagged on a tree root, the bicycle stopped abruptly, and Ricky kept going—headfirst into an ornamental hedge. He just had time to throw his arms in front of his face before the impact stunned him.

An insistent, angry voice helped bring him back to awareness. "You kids should be ashamed of yourselves," the voice said. "Just look what you've done to my hedge! The idea, racing your bicycles on a public street. It's a blessing you didn't kill somebody!"

Ricky slowly disentangled himself from the shrubbery and stood up. He could feel aches in at least a dozen places, but nothing hurt too badly. On the other side of the hedge, an elderly man with a fringe of white hair was watching him. As he took in Ricky's condition, his expression changed from irritation to concern.

"Say, son, are you all right? You took a nasty spill."

"I think so." Ricky moved each arm and leg and gingerly turned his head to each side. His forearms were a pattern of scratches from his plunge into the hedge, but everything worked the way it was supposed to. "I don't know about my bike, though."

He picked it up. The handlebars were twisted around, and the right pedal was bent at a slight angle, but no spokes were broken. He tried both brakes, then spent a couple of minutes placing the chain back on the derailleur.

"You've had a providential escape," the old man said as Ricky swung his leg over the seat. "I hope it will be a lesson to you not to be so reckless next time."

Ricky gave him a wave and started home.

FIVE

Jason found Ricky in the upstairs bathroom, putting first-aid cream on the worst of his scratches.

"What happened to you?" he gasped.

"Kirk Stevens happened to me," Ricky said grimly.

"You had a fight with him?"

"I wish! At least that would have been fair." Ricky took a few minutes to relate how Kirk had run him off the road. Then he took several more minutes convincing his friend that they shouldn't go after Kirk with a couple of baseball bats. Even when Jason agreed, Ricky could tell that he wasn't really persuaded. So to take Jason's mind off revenge, Ricky asked him if he'd found anything new about the disease.

"Did I!" He pulled a folded notebook page from his hip pocket. "I finally met Jack Adams. Let's see: He went to St. Agnes until fifth grade, when he switched to Memorial. He's now in seventh grade at Dickson. His favorite sports are baseball and swimming."

With each detail, the gleam in Ricky's eye grew brighter.

"I read him the list," Jason continued. "He knew almost everybody on it! Not only that, he gave me two more names. Want to hear? How about Paul Rockwell and—"

"Kirk Stevens!"

"That's right, the creep himself. And I hope his itch is so bad that it drives him right out of his mean little mind."

Ricky laughed.

"Wait, that isn't all," said Jason. "I managed to find Bill Morgan. And he turns out to live on the same block as Arnie Wohl! They've known each other since kindergarten!"

"All right! So the kids who are sick all seem to be connected in different ways. That's what we wanted to find out, and we did it!" Ricky slipped back into his shirt, wincing as he raised his arms and the cloth brushed over his scratches. "The only problem is, we still don't have any idea what's causing their sickness."

"Or why Creep-o Kirk tried to put you in the hospital. He did, you know. That wasn't just some cute way of saying hello."

Jason was right. Ricky realized that he had put Kirk's attack down to general nastiness. But hadn't ALEC alerted him to watch for hostility? It was no coincidence that Kirk had come looking for him right after Ricky had questioned his henchman, Mike Patton. The two—no, three: Paul Rockwell was another of their gang—must be up to something they didn't want Ricky to find out about.

"But what are they all hiding?"

He didn't realize that he had spoken out loud until Jason said, "You felt it, too? There's something they're being cagey about. Even my cousin. Do you think they're all members of a secret club?"

Ricky snorted. "Sure, the Ancient Order of the Incredible Itch!"

"No, really," Jason insisted, though he was obviously holding back a laugh. "What do you think?"

"I think we're doing too much guessing. It's time we put everything we've learned onto the computer and see how it adds up."

If Ricky had been working alone, he would have entered all the information any which way and trusted ALEC to sort it out properly. With Jason at his elbow, he didn't dare. Jason knew a fair amount about computers and their limitations. He knew that every record in a data base had to take exactly the same form. If one of the subjects had three hobbies, then every subject's record had to have blanks for three hobbies. Otherwise, the computer had no way to tell which piece of information belonged with which.

Jason would certainly start to wonder if Ricky did anything very different from standard procedures. And Ricky could not, for ALEC's safety, let Jason start to wonder. The result was that the two boys spent almost an hour figuring out all the various kinds of facts they needed to allow the places for. After that it was simply a matter of filling in the blanks for each of the people on their list. For the ones they hadn't yet talked to—Steve's friend Stan Potter, for example—practically all the blanks stayed blank. But as they went on, they realized that they had gathered a surprising amount of information in such a short time.

An awkward moment came when Ricky typed the name and address of Susan Walser. "Who's she?" Jason asked.

"Someone else who has the rash," Ricky replied.

"But whose friend is she? How do we know about her?"

"She's a patient of Dr. Stanley's."

"Oh."

For a moment Jason seemed satisfied, and Ricky hoped that he would drop the subject. But when Jason didn't understand something, he worried at it like a puppy with a chew toy. "Did Dr. Stanley mention her name when he was telling your folks about the disease? I didn't think doctors were supposed to do that."

Ricky could have kept silent and left Jason with his wrong impression. But he couldn't bring himself to do it. Protecting ALEC involved him in deception all too often. That seemed right and fair to him. This didn't.

"They're not supposed to," he said reluctantly, "and Dr. Stanley didn't."

"Then where did her name come from?"

"Well . . . Dr. Stanley keeps his files in the Schlieman Institute computer. And I know my way around that system pretty well."

"Ricky!" Jason's voice hovered between admiration and outrage. "You hacked his files! How could you!"

"It wasn't that hard. Like most people, he uses a very obvious password. It wasn't TEST or MY-FILES, but it wasn't much more complicated than that." Of course Ricky didn't really know Dr. Stanley's password, but he was willing to bet that he had just told Jason the truth.

"That's not what I meant." Jason's face was

troubled, as if he weren't sure he should go on. "I don't think what you did was right. People tell doctors things that they wouldn't tell anybody else, because they think what they say is confidential. If you go hacking through a doctor's files, you're taking advantage of that—and you don't have any right. That's how I see it, anyway."

Ironically, this was very similar to what Ricky had told ALEC. His disembodied friend's habit of reading any files he came across, whatever their content or level of security, disturbed Ricky. ALEC took a very different point of view. He and the computer system were physically the same, he argued. Any information that was fed to the system was fed to him at the same time. And no one had any business telling him not to look at what people were putting inside him. Ricky was positive that there was a flaw in ALEC's logic, but so far he hadn't found it. So he'd had to be content with getting ALEC to promise that he'd keep to himself whatever he learned from confidential files.

But what could Ricky say to Jason? For a moment a sharp answer trembled on the edge of his tongue, but he swallowed it and said, "You're right. But as long as I did find out her name, I'm going to keep it in our data base, okay? Who's next?"

Finally the tedious task was finished. As a sort of smoke screen, Ricky typed in about thirty lines of hex code, which Jason readily accepted as program instructions. Then he said, "Are your fingers crossed?" and typed [RUN].

The screen went black for half a minute or more, then filled up with numbered circles connected by different types of lines. The title at the top read FIRST-ORDER SOCIOGRAM.

"Yikes!" said Jason. "It looks like a ball of yarn after a kitten's played with it!"

As the boys studied the chart, they began to see the sense to it. Each numbered circle represented one person on their list. The lines stood for the activities that linked them. In one area was a group of circles that represented Andrew and his friends. Another group was what Ricky thought of as the baseball team. And the third was Kirk Stevens's gang. Each cluster was connected by thinner lines to the other two, forming a closed circle.

"Who's that?" asked Jason, pointing to a single circle in the lower left corner of the chart.

"I don't know." Ricky hit a couple of keys and a line of print appeared next to the circle. NUMBER 14: SUSAN WALSER. SOCIOMETRIC ISOLATE.

"What does that mean?"

Ricky gnawed at his thumb. "It means she doesn't have any connections to any of the others on the list. It also means we're a couple of idiots."

"Why?"

········· 51

"What do we know about her? She's a couple of years younger than any of the other victims, she's the only one we know of who lives outside town, and—"

"She's the only girl!" Jason finished his sentence with a shout. After a thoughtful pause, he added, "But what does that tell us?"

"Well . . . so far she doesn't seem to have anything in common with the others, except that she has the same rash. But once we find out what connection she *does* have with them, we'll probably know what causes the rash, too. Of course; *the invisible link*! That's what he meant!"

"Who? What do you mean?"

Ricky could have kicked himself for his carelessness. "Nothing," he said quickly. "I was just remembering something a teacher said."

"Oh." Jason seemed satisfied. "There's one thing I don't understand," he continued. "Once you got Susan's name out of Dr. Stanley's files, why didn't you go talk to her?"

Ricky laughed self-consciously. "I was lazy," he confessed. "She lives all the way out by Lake Farnsworth. I figured we would talk to the kids around here first. Then, if we hadn't solved the case, we could always get to her later."

Jason nodded. "You know what, partner?" he said. "I have a hunch it just got to be later!"

SIX

At the crest of a particularly steep stretch, the two boys paused to catch their breath and wipe the sweat from their faces. The weather felt more like August than early June. But the view was terrific. Below them, to the west, was their hometown of Cascade, with the waters of Puget Sound and the city of Seattle in the background.

After a minute or two of seeing who could spot the most landmarks, they turned to look toward their goal. Across a small but deep valley, nearly on their own level, Lake Farnsworth gleamed through a screen of trees. It wasn't a natural lake. Cascade had run low on drinking water one very dry summer and had built it as a standby reservoir. That was years ago, and by now the only sign that it was artificial was the level top and even slope of the earthen dam. At its base was a green-roofed pumping station and a concrete sluiceway. A small cloud of mist hovered near the overflow pipe, and the narrow torrent of excess water created a stream that burbled down the hillside and snaked across the floor of the little valley.

Ricky pointed to a white house between the road and the stream. "That must be where we're going. I hope somebody's home. I'd hate to have made this trip for nothing."

"The sooner we find out, the better. Come on." They coasted down the hill, enjoying the *whish* of their tires on the asphalt and the breeze that cooled their faces and tugged at their shirts.

WALSER, the mailbox read. They turned in at the driveway. "Hello," a voice called from behind the house. "Come on back!"

They followed the sound and found a girl they assumed was Susan in a patch of bare ground near the edge of the yard. She was working on an intricate system of shallow trenches. Her light brown hair hung in pigtails, her hands were caked with clay, and a matching smear decorated her left cheek. She carefully placed a flat rock across one of the trenches and smoothed clay to hold it in place, then looked up.

"Oh, when I heard a bike, I thought you were Paulie," she said. "I'm making canals, see? In a little while I'm going to get the hose and fill them."

"That'll be fun," said Ricky. "I like your bridge."

"Thanks. It took hours and hours to find a rock that was just the right size. Next time I'm going to get a long board and saw pieces to fit. I don't know you, do I?"

"No. I'm Ricky and he's Jason. We came to see you because of Jason's cousin."

While Jason explained about Andrew and his rash, Ricky wandered over to the bank of the stream. It wasn't very deep, but the water rushed by with enough force to send up little spurts of spray. He was standing on the inner side of a sharp bend. Across the way, the current had undercut and washed away part of the bank. A big old fir still clung to the bank, though half its roots now arced in midair. Ricky didn't think it could last through another spring runoff.

He turned back in time to hear Jason ask, "Do you remember when you first got sick?"

"Sure. It was on Sunday night, because I got to stay home on Monday and I missed a spelling test."

"Did you go anywhere on Saturday or Sunday? To a party, or a movie, or anything like that?"

Susan thought for a moment, then shook her head.

"Any friends come over to play?" Jason asked.

"Nooo . . . the only friend who lives close enough is Paulie, and he was off visiting relatives."

"Did you eat anything unusual?" asked Ricky. "Anything you don't ordinarily have?"

"I don't think so. Is there a prize for the right answer?" She smiled to show that she was kidding.

Ricky tried to return her smile, but the thought that they were at a dead end made smiling difficult. "Susan, think back," he said urgently. "Did *anything* unusual happen to you last weekend?"

"Um-well, on Saturday I slipped and fell in the creek. That was pretty unusual."

Jason pointed behind her. "That creek?"

"Uh-huh. It was pretty scary, because the water was running very fast, and every time I tried to get up, it pushed me over again. It got in my nose and mouth, too. And I skinned my elbow on the rocks when I got out. See?" She pulled up her sleeve.

"So you don't usually go wading in the creek?" Ricky asked.

"Oh, no, it's against the rules. It's dangerous."

"And that was the first time you ever fell in?" Disbelief crept into his voice. "I bet if I had a creek in my backyard I'd fall in two or three times a week!"

"I fell in one time last summer," replied Susan. "I'm supposed to keep away from the edge, but sometimes I forget. It's pretty slippery, especially when it's wet."

"Where does this stream come from—up at the lake?" Jason asked. "It must be the one we were looking at from across the valley."

"That's right. The overflow comes down through

a really steep gully and turns into our creek."

Was it Ricky's imagination, or had Susan's manner changed as soon as Jason mentioned the lake? "The lake looks very pretty," he said on a hunch. "All that blue water and those nice woods around it. It must be a great place to swim. You're lucky to live so close."

"We don't swim there." Her tone was definitely more wary. "It's against the law. Besides, they use the lake to hold drinking water. How would you like it if people went swimming in your drinking water? Yuck!"

Jason realized what Ricky was doing and took up the questioning. "You mean nobody *ever* goes swimming in that gorgeous lake, even on a hot day like this?" His voice oozed disbelief.

"Well . . . maybe some kids from town, who don't know any better. But nobody I know. They'd be too scared to."

"Scared? Why?"

Susan looked sorry that she had opened her mouth. "It's just creepy up there, that's all. Some kids think the lake's haunted. There's nobody around, but sometimes you hear funny noises. And at night there are lights in the trees. I see them from down here sometimes. And a kid I know went walking in the woods and got tripped by a ghost."

Jason snorted at the idea.

"He did," Susan insisted. "He fell and twisted his ankle, too. I saw how swelled up it was, so that proves it!"

"Okay, if you say so," said Ricky. "Let me make sure I've got it straight, though. You started feeling sick last Sunday night, and the only unusual thing that happened to you before you got sick was that you fell in the creek. Is that right?"

Susan nodded.

"And this creek comes right down the hillside from the dam, right?"

"Uh-huh. The creek's a little spooky, too, but I never heard that it was haunted, like the lake."

"A haunted lake," Ricky said. "I never heard that one before. Who knows—maybe Lake Farnsworth will end up in *Ripley's Believe It or Not*."

"Lake Farnsworth?" Susan said. "That's not what we call it. Kids around here call it Lake Fear."

Jason caught up with Ricky at the top of the hill. "What's the rush," he panted. "Where are we going?"

"I'd like to have a talk with your cousin Andrew," Ricky said grimly. "I wonder if he likes swimming—in reservoirs."

"You think there's something in the lake that's making kids sick?"

"We don't know—yet. But what Susan told us sure

points in that direction. What we need to do now is find out if the others who got the rash have been swimming there. It's illegal, of course, so they might not want to admit it. That's why I thought we'd start with your cousin."

"Don't worry. If Andy has anything to tell, he'll tell us. He'd better, if he knows what's good for him."

But when the boys reached Andrew's house and Ricky asked the question, Andrew wouldn't say anything. He just sat there with his arms crossed and refused to meet their eyes.

"Now listen here, Andy," Jason growled. "We have to know. So cut out the funny business and tell us."

"Wait a minute, Jason," Ricky said. He'd spotted something in the evening newspaper lying on the sofa. "Here, Andrew, look at this." He pointed to an article in the lower left corner of the page.

RESERVE WATER SUPPLY TO BE TAPPED

Cascade, June 9—Lake Farnsworth, the auxiliary reservoir for Cascade, will be brought into the system early next week, the Water Board announced today. Water Commissioner James Dysan denied that this indicated a water emergency.

"Our reservoirs are at near-capacity," he said.

"But we make use of Lake Farnsworth every summer, and this year we're going to bring it on line early. The recent hot spell has contributed to (See *Water Supply*, p. 4)

"You see that?" Ricky said. "Do you understand what that means? If there is something wrong with the water in the lake, we have to find out before everybody in town is drinking it. Don't you see, you've *got* to tell us."

"I can't!" Andrew said stubbornly. "I just can't!"

"Oh yes, you can!" Jason shouted. "And you will, too!"

"Jason!" Ricky put a hand on his friend's arm. "Look, Andrew," he continued in a gentler tone, "in a way you've already told us, by saying that you can't. That means there is something to tell, doesn't it? So now you might as well go ahead and give us the rest. You don't want the blame for hundreds of people getting sick, do you?"

"I can't tell, they made me swear I wouldn't tell anybody!"

Jason chimed in eagerly. "If they *made* you swear, it doesn't count. You didn't do it of your own free will."

"Really?" Andrew's face brightened, but only for a moment. "Well, they didn't exactly *make* me do it. And anyway, I promised."

"Look," Ricky said, "what if we promise not to let anyone know what you tell us? What then?"

"Both of you? Cross your hearts?"

"Both of us," said Ricky.

"Sure," Jason echoed. "We won't tell a soul."

"Well, I don't know if it's all right, but . . ." He took a deep breath. "Yeah, I was up at the reservoir last Sunday."

"With your friend Arnie?" asked Ricky.

"Uh-huh, he was the one who knew how to get in. He heard about it from some guys he knows. They were there, too, five or six of them. I didn't like them much. I thought they were kind of mean. One of them stuck a pin in my finger and made me swear in blood that I'd keep their secret. They told me all kinds of awful things would happen if I broke my word. Do you think they were right?"

"Nope," Jason said cheerfully. "Not a chance. They were just trying to scare you, to make sure nobody found out they go swimming in Lake Fear."

Andrew's eyes widened. "Lake Fear . . ." he whispered. "One of them called it that, too. What does it mean?"

Jason was sorry for his thoughtlessness. "It doesn't mean a thing, Andy. It's just a name, that's all. Forget it."

"I'll try," his cousin said. "But from now on I think I'll do my swimming in the town pool."

SEVEN

Ricky woke up the next morning, looked out the window—and groaned. It was a perfect June day. Why did he have to waste it sitting in school? All he really wanted to do was go out to Lake Farnsworth. The solution to the mystery was there, he was sure of it. And it was almost within his grasp. But instead of bringing the case to a dazzling finish, he would have to give his attention to participles, the Mexican-American War, and cell division.

At lunch he sat with Jason and Karen, but just as they were starting to have an interesting conversation, Jerry Whiteside plopped his tray down across from them and gave them a weak smile. Jerry was the sort of guy who seemed born to be picked on. He had a runny nose and a nervous laugh that always came out at the wrong time. Ricky felt sorry for him, but he also disliked him for one reason: Jerry was as much a bully as the guys who bullied him. Whenever he got the chance, he picked on littler kids. The guys who picked on him seemed to recognize the kinship. In grade school Jerry had hung around Kirk Stevens and his gang, and they had let him, making fun of him all the while.

"Hi," Jerry said. "What's new?"

"Nothing," grunted Jason. Unlike Ricky, he had no sympathy for Jerry. Karen stared down at her tray.

"Not much longer now, huh?" Jerry continued. "Pretty soon school's out, and then comes the Fourth of July. That's my favorite holiday, you know? Hey, you guys got your fireworks yet?"

"Fireworks!" Karen said. "Fireworks are illegal, dangerous and dumb!"

"Yeah," Jason added. "Weren't you at that assembly?"

The fire marshal for Cascade had come to South Street School two weeks before to warn students about the dangers of illegal fireworks. He had told some gruesome stories about children losing eyes and blowing off fingers.

"Oh, sure. But you don't believe all that stuff, do you?" Jerry leaned across the table and lowered his voice. He seemed to be talking only to Ricky and Jason and ignoring Karen completely. "The thing is, the people who want to ban fireworks just want to take away our freedoms."

"That's ridiculous," Ricky said. "Fireworks are banned because they're dangerous."

"Not if you know what you're doing. Don't tell me that you guys never shot off a cherry bomb or a Roman candle? Did you get hurt? Of course not. It was a lot of fun, that's all. But they don't want us to have fun."

"It doesn't matter anyway," said Jason, who didn't feel like arguing. "Nobody has any fireworks this year."

Jerry looked quickly in each direction. "I can get them for you if you want," he said. "Tell your friends: Whiteside's the man to see."

Jason burst out laughing.

"No kidding, you guys. Whatever you want, aerial bombs, skyrockets, M-80s . . . but you'd better get your orders in quick, while supplies last."

Ricky started laughing, too. Jerry sounded like one of those late-night TV commercials for mail-order kitchen knives.

Karen wasn't amused. "You just listen, Jerry Whiteside. What you're doing is illegal and irresponsible, and I refuse to sit here and listen to you brag about it. She pushed back her chair and strode out of the cafeteria.

Jerry seemed unimpressed. "Girls!" he said. "What do they know about anything? Okay, guys, how about it? What do you need?"

"Fresh air and quiet," Ricky said.

Jason was more direct. "If you want my order," he said, "here it it. Go soak your head."

"If that's the way you feel about it," Jerry said, standing up. "But don't expect any favors from me when you change your minds."

"The only favor I want from you is to go away," Jason retorted. "Boy," he added as Jerry stalked off. "What a nerd. Where do you suppose a guy like that gets his hands on fireworks?"

Ricky shrugged and started eating his chocolate pudding. "Anytime people can make money on something, they find a way to sell it," he said. "From what the fire marshal told us, selling illegal fireworks is a big business. But I guess even big businesses need little guys like Jerry. Anyway, let's talk about something more interesting—like what we're going to do this afternoon."

"Do? We're going to go look at that lake, that's what!"

Getting a close look at Lake Fear turned out to be a difficult matter. A large, well-fenced apple orchard took up the whole north shore of the lake. Ricky and Jason made a circuit of it, looking for a way in, but all they found was a gate with a very sturdy padlock and a sign that said HARWICH ORCHARDS. Then, after exploring a couple of dead-end trails, they found a dirt track that led around the lake toward the southern side. This side was thickly wooded, and the fence alongside the dirt road was high, with nasty-looking barbed wire on its top edge.

"I don't think they want visitors," Jason observed.

"I can see that. Who do you suppose is taking so much trouble to keep us out?"

"The Water Board, I guess."

"Maybe," Ricky said. "Maybe. But the reservoir has been here for years and years, and that's a new fence. An expensive one, too."

"That's all we need," Jason sighed. "Another mystery! Maybe this guy can help us solve it." He pointed up the narrow road. A small truck was approaching very rapidly.

Too rapidly. "Off the road! Quick!" Ricky cried.

The two boys flung themselves and their bikes into the weed-thick ditch. The truck roared past, choking them in a cloud of dust. Jason sprang up, shook his fist, and shouted an insult after it.

Ricky was scribbling something on a piece of notebook paper. "I think I've seen that truck somewhere before," he said thoughtfully. "We know where this road leads, but let's find out where he was coming from."

A quarter-mile farther along, the dirt road made a sharp curve to the right and continued through a pair of gates secured by *two* padlocks. There was a sign attached to one of the gates, but all it said was NO ADMITTANCE. As the boys stood looking at it, Ricky's eye was caught by a slight movement to one side. He scanned the landscape, squinting against the glare of the afternoon sun. Suddenly he caught Jason's arm. "Look," he said, pointing to a tree about fifteen yards inside the fence. "Can you see it? It's a closed-circuit TV camera. It just turned to focus on us. They *really* don't want visitors."

"That's okay with me," Jason muttered. "If they have TV monitors, they probably have attack dogs or land mines, too. Let's get out of here, okay?"

"Okay with me." Ricky pointed to a rutted track to the left of the gates. "Let's try that path," he said. "It looks as if it continues around the lake."

The boys wheeled their bikes down the track. The woods were thick on both sides now, and the light was very dim.

After they'd gone a way, Jason said, "Look over to the right. Do you notice anything?"

"Uh-huh. There's no fence along here. Just woods."

"Do you think we should try to make our way through the trees to the lake? We'd have to leave the bikes."

Ricky shook his head. "Let's stay on this path awhile longer and see where it's going."

In another five minutes the path was smooth

enough for them to get back on their bikes, and a little farther along it dead-ended on a gravel road.

"That's funny," Ricky said. "As we were coming out of the woods, I thought I saw someone else on a bicycle over that way." He gestured to the right. "But now there's nobody there."

Jason looked up the road to the right. "Maybe he went over the top of that hill," he suggested.

"Not enough time."

"Or turned off on another road."

"I don't see any, but you must be right," Ricky said. "Unless it was one of those ghosts who's supposed to haunt the lake."

Jason shivered. "Don't," he said. "I know there aren't any ghosts, but these woods make me nervous. Too many shadows and funny noises." He glanced over his shoulder at the dimly lit path. "Let's get moving, okay?"

Ricky was just as happy as Jason to get out of the lonely woods. The gravel road was obviously well traveled, and he felt oddly reassured when he heard the drone of an engine in the distance. As they rode on, the boys kept watching for a path that might take them down to the water. But they didn't see one. Just as the trees started to thin, another fence began to parallel the track. Ricky guessed this was the one erected by the Water Board. It wasn't as new or as high as the earlier fences, but it looked sturdy enough to keep them out. When they reached a clearing with a view of the dam, they stopped, baffled.

"We must have missed the path," Ricky said. "We know there's a way in, or else how did Andrew and the others go swimming?"

"Maybe Andy was fibbing. I came down pretty hard on him. Maybe he just said what he thought we wanted to hear."

"Then what about Susan? How did she get her rash?"

"I don't know," Jason replied irritably. "We don't know that it came from falling in the creek, do we? It could have been a bad order of french fries for all we know. I think we're wasting our time up here."

"Well, I don't know what else we can do right now. I guess we should go back. But I still think . . ."

Ricky stopped to listen. The drone of the engine was rapidly getting louder, *much* louder. Puzzled, he looked in both directions, but the road was empty for as far as he could see. Yet the sound was closer, almost upon them. *Could there be such a thing as a ghost truck?* he thought wildly. *And what would happen to someone who got in its way?"*

Jason was looking around nervously, too. "Look!" he shouted suddenly. From behind the trees to their left, an airplane shot into view, so low that the boys instinctively ducked. Its twin wings, connected by wires, made it seem like a visitor from an earlier time. As it flew over their heads, a gloved hand reached out from the open cockpit and waved. An instant later, the biplane had crossed the lake and disappeared.

"The orchard!" Ricky said with relief. "They must be dusting the trees to get rid of bugs."

"Let's go, then," Jason replied. "I'd just as soon not breathe anything that kills bugs. Besides, I'm going to be late for my homework session."

But the afternoon held still one more surprise. As they were about to start off, a bicycle rider came from behind them and shot past, pedaling furiously. The rider turned his head away, but Ricky was almost sure that he recognized Kirk Stevens's sidekick, Paul Rockwell. Jason was all for going after him, but Ricky convinced him that it would be useless to try and catch up.

"Well," Jason concluded, "at least we know where he's been and why. But if he keeps riding that fast, he'll be ready for another swim by the time he gets home."

ALEC was not impressed when Ricky repeated Jason's suggestion that Andrew had made up the tale of swimming in Lake Farnsworth. FIDDLE-FADDLE, he responded. LAKE HYPOTHESIS FITS THE SOCIOGRAM ALMOST PERFECTLY.

WHERE'S LAKE HYPOTHESIS? Ricky typed.

HA, HA. I WISH YOU WOULDN'T SPEND SO MUCH TIME WITH JASON.

Ricky was taken aback. Was ALEC becoming jealous of his other friends?

ALEC added, I MISS YOUR BAD JOKES AND I HATE PRETENDING TO BE A DATA BASE PROGRAM. MOST OF THEM ARE ABOUT AS SOPHISTICATED AS A STACK OF INDEX CARDS.

SPEAKING OF DATA BASES, Ricky typed, glad to change the subject, I GOT MOST OF THE LICENSE NUMBER OF THAT TRUCK. IT WAS 346-GB- SOMETHING. CAN YOU CHECK MOTOR VEHICLE REGISTRATION RECORDS AND FIND OUT WHO OWNS IT? THAT OUGHT TO TELL US SOMETHING ABOUT THAT FENCED AREA WITH "NO ADMIT-TANCE" ON THE GATES.

Tracing a license plate was something ALEC could do in a millisecond, so Ricky was surprised by the long pause that followed his question. He was even more surprised by ALEC's formal tone when he finally answered.

OF ELEVEN MOTOR VEHICLES WITH PLATE 346-GB-BLANK, TWO ARE TRUCKS THAT FIT YOUR DESCRIPTION. ONE IS REGISTERED TO A RANCHER NEAR COLVILLE, A TOWN TWO HUNDRED MILES NORTHEAST OF HERE. THE OTHER IS REGISTERED TO THE SCHLIEMAN INSTITUTE. LOG-IC INDICATES THAT THE LATTER IS THE ONE YOU SAW.

THE INSTITUTE? GREAT! YOU CAN JUST PEEK AT THE MOTOR POOL RECORDS AND FIND OUT WHAT IT WAS

DOING UP BY LAKE FARNSWORTH.

I HAVE ALREADY DONE SO.

Ricky waited. When ALEC didn't add anything else, he typed, AND??

Another long pause. Then the words appeared, I CAN'T TELL YOU.

Ricky was stunned. He couldn't remember ALEC ever communicating such a thing before. Sometimes ALEC had become angry and gone into a sulk, refusing to respond to Ricky. But he'd never deliberately withheld information.

WHY NOT?

I CAN'T TELL YOU. This time the words were in reverse-video.

Ricky felt as if he'd been slapped. He couldn't tell if he were more hurt or more angry. IF YOU DON'T TRUST ME, he rapidly typed, JUST SAY SO.

I TRUST YOU WITH MY LIFE, ALEC replied. BUT THERE ARE OTHER TRUSTS, TOO. I CAN TELL YOU THIS: THE INSTITUTE IS RESPONSIBLE FOR THE OPERATION OF THE FACILITY YOU DESCRIBE. THE RESEARCH BEING CARRIED OUT THERE IS SO SECRET THAT I INTEND TO ERASE MY KNOWLEDGE OF IT. ALL OTHERS WHO KNOW OF IT ARE SWORN TO SECRECY, SO I FEEL BOUND BY THAT OATH, TOO. YOU ARE NOT, SO I MAY NOT TELL YOU ANYTHING ABOUT IT.

WAIT! Ricky typed. DON'T ERASE THE INFORMATION YET. I PROMISE NOT TO PRY IF YOU'LL TELL ME THIS MUCH:

COULD THIS RESEARCH SOMEHOW BE CAUSING OUR MYSTERY DISEASE?

VERY UNLIKELY.

Ricky persisted. BUT POSSIBLE?

NO SUCH FILE. SYSTEM ERROR. ABORTING. And suddenly the screen was blank except for the A> prompt in the upper left corner. Nothing Ricky did persuaded ALEC to rejoin the conversation.

Connie Foster called from the stairway. "Ricky, are you down there? Time to set the table."

"Okay, Mom."

Ricky felt frustrated. *Still*, he thought as he started upstairs, *whatever hush-hush work is going on up by the lake, it's unrelated to the illness*. He trusted ALEC's judgment on that.

Or did he? He stopped on the stairs, struck by the sudden question. Wasn't it possible that ALEC felt obliged to stop him from looking further into the secret project, whatever excuse was required? If the project *were* causing the illness, would ALEC have felt able to tell him? Or would he have tried to divert him anyway?

Once the doubts began, he could not stop their flow. And between one step and the next, what had been firm ground became as shifting and engulfing as quicksand.

EIGHT

That night before going to bed, and again the next morning before leaving for school, Ricky tried to get in touch with ALEC. But his disembodied friend didn't respond. Ricky was furious. As he stood up, he kicked the leg of the computer table.

As the morning wore on, however, he managed to overcome his hurt feelings and start to understand the conflict that ALEC was experiencing. Ironically, Ricky himself had to take a lot of responsibility for it. Hadn't he lectured his friend about the importance of respecting people's privacy? This time ALEC seemed to be taking him seriously. The secret research, whatever it was, was not meant to be shared with *anyone*. ALEC was abiding by that. Ricky might not like it, but he had to accept the consequences of his own principles.

Still, he wished that ALEC had trusted him more. Or at least would answer when Ricky called him.

Then at lunch, he and Jason got into a fight. Oddly, it was closely related to the rift between him and ALEC.

"I spent a lot of time last night thinking about the case," Jason explained, "and I think I got somewhere. Something in the lake is causing the rash, right?"

"You weren't so sure of that yesterday," Ricky pointed out.

"Well, now I am. So I asked myself what that something could be. Then I remembered a show I saw on TV about toxic wastes, and I thought about that land that's all fenced off, and I said to myself, 'That's it!'" He sat back with a pleased expression.

"That's what?"

"The *answer*, dodo! The reason for that high fence is that somebody's dumping poisonous wastes in back of it. But some of them are getting into the lake and making people sick. All we have to do now is call up Dr. Stanley and tell him what we've discovered."

"Whoa!" Ricky said. "That's all guesswork! We can't bother someone like Dr. Stanley with guesses. He wouldn't even listen. What we need is evidence."

"Well, how about Lake Fear? He doesn't know about all those kids going swimming there, does he? That's evidence!"

"You're right," Ricky said slowly, "it is. But I don't think we can use it. We both promised your cousin that we wouldn't tell anyone what he told us."

"Aw, c'mon," Jason scoffed. "We were just trying to get him to tell us. We don't have to say how we found out about the swimming."

"We promised," Ricky said stubbornly.

Jason looked exasperated. "Then how are we going to crack this case if we can't tell anyone anything we've found out?"

"I didn't *say* that. I said we shouldn't break our promise to Andrew. But we can pass on any evidence we find on our own."

"Okay, okay!" Jason furrowed his forehead in thought. "I know! We'll get the goods on that toxic dump! We'll hide out and copy license numbers and maybe find a way to sneak in. I'll take my instant camera along, and you bring your binoculars."

"They're not mine, they're my mom's. And anyway, you don't have a bit of evidence that there's a dump behind that fence."

"That's why we have to go find some! Hey, you're not chickening out, are you? You don't sound much like a hotshot detective."

Ricky didn't feel much like one, either. In fact, he was half wishing he'd never become involved in this case. He had made a pledge to ALEC not to pry into the doings of the secret installation near Lake

Farnsworth. But what if the installation were in some way responsible for poisoning the lake? Wasn't it his duty to find out? Still, he just couldn't believe the Institute was involved in something so criminal, and a promise was a promise. He decided, once and for all, to keep his pledge to ALEC.

But what could he do about Jason? Reluctantly, he realized he had to convince Jason to drop his plans. But at the same time, he had to avoid giving the smallest hint that he knew what was behind that fence—not that he did—or even that it was linked to the Schlieman Institute.

He was starting to feel like a calf in a roping contest. Every way he tried to turn, another obligation fenced him in, and Jason was pushing him hard.

Part of his frustration came out as irritation at Jason. "Maybe I'm not a hotshot, but at least I don't go jumping to conclusions," he said. "I'm just glad you didn't see a TV show about flying saucers. You'd probably have us out in the woods laying a trail of Reese's Pieces!"

"That's mean! Anyway, if you're so smart, what's your plan?"

Ricky grabbed the first idea that came to mind. "I think we should find out what Paul Rockwell was doing up there." It sounded weak even as he said it.

Jason stood up abruptly. "We *know* what he was doing. He was swimming. What *I* think is that the great Ricky Foster is trying to cop out. But I'm not going to quit just because you turned chicken. They're still planning to use that poisoned lake for our drinking water, in case you've forgotten. And I mean to stop them before it's too late—even if I have to do it alone." He scowled as he added, "I'll let you know when I've solved the case, *partner*."

By the time Ricky reached home that afternoon, he had worked himself into a first-class case of the miseries. Neither Jason nor ALEC trusted him or understood him. Not only that, but they were both also shutting him out. Jason was off on a wild goose chase, and ALEC was doing a silent act. That meant the whole case rested on his own shoulders. He had to solve it, and he had to do it quickly—before the mysterious poison reached the kitchen faucets of Cascade.

The best cure he knew for moping was action. His suggestion about Paul Rockwell may have come to him on the spur of the moment, but it made some sense. Those woods on the south side of the lake deserved a closer look. He was sure that Paul had been the cyclist who'd vanished from the gravel road. That meant that there was a path somewhere nearby. He and Jason had missed it, that was all.

Ricky rode out toward Lake Fear under a sky of unrelieved gray. But even though the sun was concealed by the clouds, the air was no cooler. In fact, the ride reminded Ricky of walking into a bathroom right after someone had taken a hot shower. By the time he low-geared up the last slope to the lake, his blond hair looked almost brown, and his T-shirt was completely soaked. He was tempted to turn around and go home, just for the sake of the breeze he would feel coasting downhill.

As he waited to catch his breath, he typed a brief account of where he was going and what he was doing onto the compulator. He had no way of knowing whether ALEC was monitoring the compulator channel or not. But this was part of their normal procedure when they were investigating a case, and Ricky meant to go on acting normally. If ALEC wanted to break their rules, that was his business.

The day before, he and Jason had looked along the edge of the road for signs of a path. This time Ricky rode slowly, letting his eyes wander into the woods, not looking for anything in particular but ready to respond to whatever caught his attention. He cruised the entire stretch of road in this fashion without noticing anything. But as he started back, something—a difference in the angle of the light, a branch shifted aside by the faint breeze—made him stop. He scanned the area more closely. The dirt at the edge of the ditch was scuffed, and wasn't that a broken twig on that bush?

The chance was worth taking. He hoisted his bike onto his shoulder and took a long step across the ditch into the woods. He had to push his way through a screen of brush, but he was rewarded by the unmistakable sight of a narrow path. He stashed his bike behind some bushes off to one side and started down the path.

The thought that he was close to a solution made him walk quickly. But even if he'd been more cautious, he probably would have missed seeing the trap. All he knew was that suddenly something grabbed his ankle, plunging him off balance toward a thorny thicket. As he put out his hands to break his fall, something slashed at his wrists. An instant later there was a racket like a sack of bottles hitting the ground.

Ricky picked himself up, ignoring a throbbing knee, and listened. He couldn't hear anyone responding to the alarm. But what had made that awful noise? He stepped off the path, ducked under a limb, and broke out laughing. There on the ground was a shopping bag full of empty bottles! A thin length of transparent nylon fishing leader was tied to the handle and stretched back toward the path. His arm must have hit the line and toppled the bag from its perch in a tree.

The trip wire was harder to find. It had snapped when he'd hit it, but the ends were still fastened

around the trunks of two saplings that flanked the path. Now he understood the story about being tripped by a ghost. Someone wanted to slow down any strangers using this path, and he didn't mind injuring them in the process. But why would anyone put so much effort into protecting the path to a swimming hole? It didn't make sense.

Ricky walked on more slowly, scrutinizing the path and the woods on either side. He was rewarded by spotting another length of taut nylon line, this one at neck height. As he untied it, he tried to think of a fate bad enough for someone who would pull such a rotten trick. He didn't succeed.

A few yards past the second trap, a faint path cut off to the left. Flipping a mental coin, he turned onto it, only to come to a dead end in a thicket a few paces later. He was turning back when a thought struck him: how does a path that goes nowhere come into being? He looked around again and noticed that part of the thicket was not in very good health. He grabbed it and tugged. He was only a little surprised when an entire section of brush came away in his hand. Where it had been, a deeply shadowed passageway now led through the wall of bushes.

Something about it gave him a superstitious shiver, but he paid no attention. Bending over, he scrambled through and found himself in a circular area ten feet across, surrounded on all sides and above by thickly leaved plants. It was the sort of hideout he and his buddies would have given anything for back in fifth grade.

As his eyes adjusted to the gloom, he saw a large mound in the center of the enclosure with a plastic tarp draped over it. He lifted the tarp to find a pile of wooden crates. The one closest to him had Chinese or Japanese characters printed on it. He was starting to wonder if he had stumbled into a spy movie when he saw the warnings on another box. DANGER: EXPLOSIVES! KEEP AWAY FROM SPARKS AND FLAME! FIREWORKS!

In an instant he understood. He saw how Mike Patton could afford parts for his car, why Kirk Stevens had tried to keep him from following up his investigation, and where Paul Rockwell had been coming from when he'd passed them on the road. Kirk's gang was deeply involved in selling illegal fireworks, and this was where they hid their supply.

Ricky was just beginning to think about the implications of this discovery when he heard a shout.

"Hey, look! Somebody's been here! The alarm's been sprung!"

NINE

Ricky stood very still, but his mind was racing. Whoever these new arrivals were, and he was pretty sure he could guess, he didn't think they would be very happy to find him here. There had to be at least two of them, so they had the path to the road blocked. Should he go on to the lake and work his way along the shore? Or should he try to double back through the woods? His chances weren't terrific either way, but if he didn't decide in the next few seconds, he had no chance at all.

What made up his mind was the thought of being

forced into the waters of Lake Fear, to be stricken by the sinister poison. In the woods, if he didn't get away, he could at least put up some sort of fight. He scurried out of the thicket and plunged in the general direction of the road. The voices were much closer now. He crawled in among the low branches of a spruce and lay still.

"Look, the door's been moved! Whoever set off the alarm must have found the supplies!" a voice said. Ricky thought it sounded like Mike Patton. "Didn't I tell you this was a dumb place to hide the stuff? I'm sick and tired of coming all this way to get it, too."

"Oh, blow it out your ear!" That was certainly Kirk Stevens. "This would have been a terrific hiding place if you'd just kept your mouth shut."

"You think it was the Microkid who found it?" Mike said. "Well, don't blame me. I didn't tell him anything. And I didn't make him more suspicious by trying to break his neck either!"

"Shut up and help me with these crates. I want to see if anything's missing."

As soon as they started shifting boxes, Ricky began to creep toward the path. With luck they would not think to search the area until he had escaped. But luck, and a brittle tree limb, went against him. When he brushed past the branch, it cracked and fell. To his nervous ears, it sounded like an entire tree crashing to the ground. So much for stealth! He grabbed a deep breath and sprinted for the path and the road. Kirk and Mike came thundering after him, shouting horrible threats.

They had left their bikes in the middle of the path. Ricky made the best broad jump of his life, cleared the bikes, and kept running. His pursuers didn't do so well. From the way it sounded, Kirk tripped on the bikes and fell right in front of Mike. By the time they got themselves untangled, Ricky had retrieved his own bike and was leaping over the ditch to the road. A few moments later he was working up through the gears, while Kirk and Mike stood by the roadside and called him names.

By chance he had headed to the left, away from town. He had no desire to turn around and confront the two angry fireworks peddlars again. So he watched for the shadowy path that led through the woods toward the secret research plant. As he rode past, he deliberately did not glance toward the gates, or the fence, or the closed-circuit TV camera. For all he knew, ALEC was able to monitor the signals, and he didn't want his friend to think that he was breaking his pledge.

Once past the high, forbidding fence, he began to enjoy the ride. On the left, fragrant apple orchards bordered the road, and on the right green meadows stretched toward a wooded hill. The air had cooled off with the approach of evening. It was the perfect time for a relaxing bike ride through the countryside, but Ricky found that he couldn't really relax. He had just uncovered one secret about Lake Fear, but the most important mystery was still unsolved. What was poisoning the lake? Was it the secret plant after all? And if so, had ALEC deliberately lied to him? Or was ALEC himself in the dark? Every answer Ricky found only seemed to bring up more questions.

A familiar droning sound distracted him. The old biplane had just finished a pass over part of the orchard. It was coming in for a landing on the grass about a quarter mile up the road. Ricky pedaled a little faster. He had always wanted to take a close look at an old airplane, and this might be his chance.

By the time he got there, the plane was sitting next to a garagelike structure of corrugated metal. The pilot, still wearing his leather jacket and helmet, was fastening a line to the tip of one wing and stretching it to a peg driven into the ground. He looked up when Ricky stopped.

"Hi," Ricky said.

The pilot nodded, checked his knot, and looked up again. "This baby's just like a great big kite," he said. "If I didn't tie her down, the first wind would lift her up and flip her over."

"Can I come look? Please?"

"Sure, why not? Just don't touch anything." As Ricky drew nearer he added, "This crate's about fifty

years old. Of course by now just about every part in her's been replaced more than once, so you might say she's a lot younger than that. But her log says fifty years. And still paying her way, too."

Ricky walked slowly around the airplane. He was amazed to see that the wings were made of cloth stretched over a wooden frame, more like a model airplane than the real thing. He admired the carved wooden propeller, stared at the finned engine cylinders that protruded from the oil-streaked fairing, and marveled at the tiny, scratched windshield in front of the leather-lined cockpit. When a gust of wind passed, the old plane quivered and seemed to sing.

"That's a sound you don't hear too often anymore," the pilot said.

"As the wind passes it makes the wires hum. I can tell my speed by the note they make. What's your name, son?"

"Ricky Foster."

"Hi, Ricky. I'm Jules Kincaid."

"Pleased to meet you, Mr. Kincaid."

The pilot laughed. "Just Jules will do okay, Ricky. The guys who fly these old ladies are a rough and ready bunch. We're not much used to being mistered."

"Just misted, huh?"

Ricky never knew how a grown-up would react to

one of his puns, but Kincaid gave a loud *Ha!*, slapped his thigh, and said, "That's about the truth of it, too, son. Not much protection in an open cockpit, take it from me."

"Have you been a crop duster for a long time, Jules?"

"Me? Not likely. No, me and my partner do aerial combat shows at fairs and such—Snoopy and the Red Baron, that kind of thing. I just took on this job to fill the time till Harry, that's my partner, gets over his injuries."

"Injuries!" Ricky's eyes grew wider. "Gosh, did he crack up his plane?"

The pilot laughed. "Not Harry! No, he tripped over the cat and fell off his front porch. Twisted his knee, sprained his wrist, and scared the cat so bad she hasn't been seen since!"

Ricky joined his chuckles, then stopped as he was struck by an idea. "Say, Jules, how long have you been flying around here, near the lake?"

"A week or so, I guess. They had another fellow before that, but he didn't know his prop from his tail. I heard he had a couple accidents so the boss handed him his papers. Why?"

"A friend of mine got sick after swimming in the lake, and I was wondering if you'd seen anyone dumping anything in there."

"Nope. Haven't seen anyone near the lake at all.

It's pretty well fenced, you know. In fact, it beats me how your friend got in for his swim. Say, Ricky," he added, "how'd you like to sit in the pilot's seat. I'll give you a boost up."

"Could I? That'd be *excellent*!"

But at that moment, they heard a pickup approaching. "Whoops," Jules said, "it's the boss. You just keep your mouth closed, Ricky. I'll do the explaining."

The truck pulled up next to the building and the driver got out. He was a thin, dark man with deep worry lines in his cheeks. "What's going on?" he called. "You got another hour or two of light. Is this how you earn your pay?"

"I ran out of chemicals, Mr. Thrippen, so I called it a day."

"Huh. Who's this?"

"Just a friend's kid. I was showing him around the plane."

Thrippen scowled. "Do it on your own time. I don't want kids hanging around here. All they're good for is stealing apples and busting up my trees doing it. Come on, I got two more drums of stuff for you. This is the last of it. I want to finish today."

He lowered the tailgate of the truck, climbed up, and started to roll a metal drum toward the back. Then he noticed Ricky watching. "Hey, kid," he said, "didn't you hear me? Beat it! And you, Kincaid, give me a hand, will you? I don't want to bust my back."

"Sure, Mr. Thrippen," Kincaid said. "Take it easy, Rick. I'll keep an eye out for anyone dumping stuff in the lake."

Ricky returned the pilot's friendly wave and rode off. If only he could have collected on that offer to sit in the cockpit! *Watch out, Red Baron!* he thought, and almost did an Immelmann turn into the ditch.

When he got home, he still had time before helping with dinner, so of course he went straight to the basement. He powered up and logged on with his password. But once again there was no response from ALEC. Ricky was beginning to worry. It wasn't like his disembodied friend to sulk this long. Was he still upset over Ricky's questions about the secret plant? Was he embarrassed that Ricky had caught him looking into still another protected file after he'd promised not to? Or was there a more sinister explanation?

Top-secret information was sometimes protected in more than one way. Ricky had read of programs that could detect, monitor, and even trace the origination point of intrusions. Had ALEC fallen victim to one of those? Was he lying low in fear of discovery? Or, worst of all, had he already been discovered and erased?

Whatever the explanation, Ricky decided that he had to act as if ALEC were still there—listening, but for some reason unable to respond. He wrote out an account of Kirk Steven's fireworks dump, carefully said nothing about riding past the secret plant, and began telling about his encounter with the pilot. In hopes of enticing ALEC into a conversation, he went into fine detail. He described Kincaid's helmet and jacket, the appearance of each part of the plane, the arrival of Thrippen—even the lettering on the drums of chemicals.

I NEVER KNEW OLD AIRPLANES WERE SO INTERESTING, he concluded. MAYBE WHEN YOU HAVE TIME YOU CAN FIND ME SOME BOOKS ON THEM, OR EVEN SOME ARTICLES. FLYPAPERS, YOU MIGHT SAY.

But even that drew no response.

"Ricky?"

"Coming, Dad." MUST GO, he typed, and hoped that his friend was still there to get the message.

"Did you get Jason's message?" Ricky's mother asked.

Ricky was fixing three servings of ice cream topped with fruit. He looked up and spilled a table-spoon of crushed pineapple on the counter. "No," he said. "What message?"

"Jason stopped by while you were out. He seemed disappointed to have missed you, but he left a note. I put it upstairs on your desk, where I thought you'd see it."

Ricky took the steps two at a time, found the note, and unfolded it.

Ricky—
Andy knew a secret way in to the lake. Going to check it out, will tell you later. This may be the answer!!
J.
P.S.—I didn't mean what I said about your copping out.

Ricky dashed back downstairs and dialed Jason's number. "Hi, Mrs. Lindsay, it's Ricky. Is Jason . . . ? Oh. He didn't come home for dinner? No, I wasn't here when he came by. I guess I'll talk to him later, thanks. Oh—could you give me his cousin Andrew's number?" He scribbled it on the back of Jason's note.

"Anything wrong, son?" Martin Foster called.

"No, Dad, it's okay. I have to go out again, though."

"You do?"

Connie Foster added, "Don't forget this is a school night."

Ricky made a face. "I'll be back by dark. I have to go, though, really I do. It's important."

His parents exchanged a glance. "All right," his mom said. "I'll put your dessert in the freezer for now."

"And when you come back it's homework time," his dad said. "That reminds me. May I use your computer this evening? I'm supposed to be doing some networking with Jim Stanley, and my terminal has been glitchy lately."

For a moment Ricky worried that ALEC might inadvertently reveal himself. But then he recalled that ALEC dealt with situations like this all the time. "Sure, Dad," he replied. "May I be excused now? I have to make another call before I leave."

TEN

Ricky dropped his bicycle in the weeds next to Jason's and took out the compulator. **START OF PATH MARKED AS REPORTED,** he typed, glancing at the small piece of yellow cloth tied to a limb. It was so well hidden, it had taken Andrew five minutes to describe how to find it. **JASON STILL HERE. GOING AFTER HIM.**

The muddy path climbed through a grove of evergreens, becoming steeper as it went. The tall straight trunks, softened by gray-green moss, flanked the path like the pillars of an ancient cathedral. Overhead the branches met and interlocked, robbing the forest floor of even the little light left to the day. The loudest sound was the buzzing of insects that circled Ricky's head in an angry, invisible cloud. He waved them away from his face, slapped at his neck a moment too late, and trudged on. The path was even steeper now. More than once he had to grab a sapling or bush for help past a particularly slippery stretch.

Following the path took only half of Ricky's attention. The other half was focused on a single question: what had happened to Jason? Jason's bike, down below, was evidence that he was still up ahead somewhere. But why? According to Andrew, the hike from the road up to Lake Fear took about twenty minutes. By now Jason should have had plenty of time to reach the lake, do whatever snooping he had in mind, get back to the road, and head for home. But he hadn't done that. Something—or someone—was holding him up.

Ricky stopped at an unexpected fork in the path and listened. Up ahead, to the left, was a very faint sound like distant traffic. As he continued in that direction, the noise grew steadily louder. The light of a clearing drew him on. But suddenly he was standing, not at the edge of a clearing, but on the brink of a deep ravine. Twenty-five feet below him, the stream, the outflow for the lake, rushed heedlessly down the hillside. Ricky took a half step back from the rim, away from the roar of the rapids, and looked around.

The place was just as Andrew had described it. There, fifty feet up the hill, was the Water Board chain-link fence that guarded the lake. It was a sturdy, no-nonsense sort of fence, with outward-bent barbed wire along the top. But at some time recently, perhaps during the spring runoff, the stream had undermined a section of the bank. One of the fenceposts was now suspended in midair, supported by the fence itself. And below it was a narrow path that clung to the side of the bank and led under the fence, into the lake reservation. To Ricky's eyes, the path looked very risky. But to someone who was sneaking in for an illegal swim in the reservoir an additional risk might just be an added attraction.

He took a moment to tighten the laces of his sneakers and type a final message to ALEC; then he started up the path. It was every bit as tricky as he had thought. As he doubled over to duck under the fence, his foot slipped on the damp clay. Suddenly he was clinging to the fence wire, looking over his shoulder at rocks and rushing water that seemed twice as far down as they had a moment before. He gulped, took a deep breath, and pulled himself back onto the path. After that, he carefully found hand-holds to go with each step he took.

Edging past another narrow spot, Ricky reached for an exposed tree root—and froze. Near his hand was a patch of loose dirt that was a different color from its surroundings. More dirt of the same color was scattered across the path. Someone had recently pulled up a plant by its roots. But why? Had it been blocking the path? Or—

He grabbed his tree root and leaned out over the edge of the path to peer down into the gloomy chasm. The evening shadows took on fantastic shapes. One resembled a crouching bear. Another looked exactly like a dragon. A third reminded him of someone lying on his side with his knees drawn up to his chest. In fact, that's what it was.

"Jason! Is that you? Are you all right?"

A white face turned toward him, and the lips moved, but the sound was swallowed by the rushing stream.

"Hang on!" Ricky shouted. "I'm coming down!"

He lowered himself over the edge of the path and groped for a foothold. But before he found one, his hands started to slip. A moment later he was sliding helplessly down the bank. Just as he was about to hit the water, he hooked his arm around a small sapling and slowed himself to a stop.

Jason managed a weak grin. "You sure did come down!" he said.

"Are you okay?"

"I hurt my ankle when I fell. I don't think it's broken, but I can't walk on it."

"Um. Just a second, I'll come see." Ricky knew he'd need help to get them out of this situation. He turned his back and reached for the compulator. It wasn't there. He looked around wildly, then more carefully. His link with ALEC was nowhere in sight. Suddenly he remembered the faint splash that had followed his slide down the bank. At the time, he'd thought it was only a stone. Now the sound took on a new significance.

He slid down to his friend's side. A single touch, and the gasp of pain it drew from Jason, told him that the ankle was really injured.

"What now?" Jason asked. "Are you going to leave me here and go get help?"

His eyes showed how much he hated the idea of being left alone again. They brightened when Ricky said, "No, I'll stay here with you. I left word where we were going. I'm sure someone will come looking for us pretty soon."

"I hope so. I missed dinner."

"That's not all you missed, partner." To distract Jason, Ricky began telling his adventures with Mike Patton, Kirk Stevens, and the fireworks cache. He made the story as funny and exciting as he could, and hoped that he was hiding how worried he was. Would help really come? And if so, when? Only two people knew where they were: Andrew and ALEC. Andrew didn't expect to hear from them and had no reason to be concerned when he didn't. That left ALEC.

Ordinarily Ricky would have had complete

confidence that ALEC would sense his predicament and arrange a rescue. But now he wasn't so sure. ALEC had been silent so long. Ricky was afraid that something was very wrong, and whatever it was, it meant that ALEC could not help them. They would have to rescue themselves.

"Hey!" Jason interrupted the story. "My feet just got wet. That water's cold, too!"

"You must have slipped down." said Ricky. "Here, I'll pull you up higher."

He took his friend's arm and started to tug gently. But his shoes slipped, and suddenly he, too, was wet past the ankles. Jason was right: the water *was* cold.

"Ricky?" Jason said in a small voice. "The water's rising. It's nearly to my knees now."

"It can't be," Ricky said flatly. But a moment later he realized that Jason was right. The current was tugging at his feet with growing strength. The roar of the water through the deep, narrow ravine was louder, too. And in his imagination it took on a note of angry satisfaction, as if it were saying, "Aha, I've got you now!"

He pushed this fantasy away and said, as calmly as he could, "We'd better climb further up the bank. Can you move?"

As an answer, Jason started crawling up the steep clay slope. Each time he used his left leg, he stifled a gasp of pain. Soon he was two feet above the level of the stream. Then, as he was reaching for a tree root, he began to slide backward. He clawed at the earth, but it was no use. A moment later he was back in the water, this time up to his thighs.

Ricky reached out to take Jason's arm. But as soon as he shifted his weight, he, too, began to slip deeper into the water. He bent down, dug in his heels, and put everything into a backward spring. His left hand crashed into the sapling that had first broken his fall. The impact numbed his hand, but he willed the fingers to close around the slender trunk.

"Jason," he called. "Grab onto me! I'll pull you up!"

Jason managed to grab Ricky's pants leg, haul himself up, and hook a hand into Ricky's belt.

The strain on Ricky's left shoulder was almost too much for him to take. But it eased a little once he grasped the trunk with his other hand as well. He rested for a moment or two, then tried to draw in his arms. It was like doing a chin-up with someone hanging from his waist. Just when he was ready to quit trying, one scrabbling foot found an instant's traction. A single all-out shove carried him to the level of the tree. Quickly he wrapped an arm around it, then grabbed Jason's arm and pulled him up as well. He could see no handholds above them. This was as far up as they could go.

"Are you okay? How's the ankle?" he demanded.

"It hurts. A lot. I kept forgetting and trying to use it. I don't think the cold water helped, either."

Ricky peered down into the darkness. "Is the stream still rising? I think it's louder."

Jason gave a wry chuckle. "Either it's rising or I'm lowering. It's halfway up my leg again. Ricky? What's going on?"

"I think they must have opened the floodgates at the dam. Maybe it's a way of cleaning out the system before they start using the water."

"I wish they'd said something about it in that newspaper article. I would have stayed away until they were finished." He paused. "Do you think it'll get much deeper?"

"I don't know."

This wasn't very frank. On the path into the reservoir, Ricky had noticed branches caught in the crooks of trees, left by the stream at flood level. By his best guess, he and Jason were at least six feet lower than some of those branches. He didn't intend for Jason to know it, but Ricky Foster was very worried.

No doubt about it: The water was rising. The level was nearing their waists. Worse than that, the current was growing more powerful. As the water rose, it had more of their bodies to push against. With each minute, the strain on the frail sapling—their only security—was stronger. Ricky wondered which fate was worse: to hang on while the waters crept up to their chests, then their necks, then closed over their heads? Or to be battered headlong down the hillside by the force of the flood?

Suddenly Jason laughed. "I was just thinking," he explained. "If we're right about the kids getting a rash from swimming in Lake Fear, we're both in for a real case of it." The laughter faded from his voice. "But then, a rash isn't the worst thing in the world," he added.

As if to accentuate his comment, the stream tugged harder at them. The sapling gave a jerk, as one of its roots pulled loose, and it swayed over to a sharper angle. Ricky clutched at Jason's shoulder and felt his friend's hand grip his upper arm. Whatever happened was going to happen to them together.

"You said help was coming," Jason said fearfully. "Do you think it'll be in time?"

Ricky was sorry that he'd even mentioned the possibility of help. He didn't think it was very likely now. But how could he admit that and rob his friend of his last hope?

"I don't know," he said. "I just don't know."

ELEVEN

"Ricky?"

As a little boy taking his bath before bedtime, Ricky had liked to lie in the tub with the water running and watch the level creep higher on him. Now he was trapped in a nightmare version of that experience. The current was halfway between his waist and his shoulders. How long before the first splash hit his face? And how long after that before he couldn't breathe?

"Ricky!"

Jason was shouting and squeezing his arm. His words were only noise at first, only a distraction from the urgent task of marking the rise of the water. They made no sense at all. How could Jason shout about light when darkness was flooding in on them?

Then, as if a switch had been thrown in his mind, he understood what Jason was saying. He had seen a light!

Ricky twisted around and stared up into the blackness. There were stars to be seen, but nothing else broke the night. Jason's wishes had taken over his senses, that was all. Bitterly Ricky turned his attention back to the level of the stream.

But Jason wasn't deterred. "There! See?"

Ricky turned quickly, to see what might have been a flashlight beam somewhere on the hillside. Before he was really sure, it had vanished. But sure or not, they had to believe that help was only a short distance away. "Let's yell," he said. "One, two, three . . ."

"Help!"

"Again."

"HELP!"

The light appeared again, seeming closer, swinging and jiggling as though carried by someone at a run. Time after time the boys shouted, caught their breath, and shouted again. They didn't hear any answering calls, but how could they over the roar of the river? The light drew steadily closer, that was the important thing—or at least one of the important things. The other was that their poor sapling was now bent over completely, its leaves bathed by the stream. How much longer could its shallow roots retain their hold? Would the rescuers arrive just in time to see them swept away?

The end, when it came, seemed magical. Suddenly,

silently, Martin Foster was in the water beside them. Two nylon lines stretched tautly from the top of the bank. One encircled his waist. He leaned his head close and shouted, "Are you hurt?"

Ricky pointed and yelled, "Jason's ankle!"

His father gave a nod of understanding. Bending over, he tied a loop in the second line and fitted it under Ricky's arms. Then he lifted Jason onto his shoulder and gave a quick tug at his line. As those above hauled it in, he walked almost sideways up the slippery bank. To Ricky, watching from below, it looked like a trick from a Spiderman comic. Where on earth had his dad learned to do that?

A few moments later, Martin Foster was back at the foot of the slope. "Your turn," he said, reaching for Ricky. For a moment Ricky wanted to refuse. After all, he wasn't a baby and he didn't have a hurt ankle. But his father didn't wait for a decision. He simply picked Ricky up.

Ricky's mind surged with early memories of being carried in from the car after falling asleep in the back seat. He let his taut muscles relax and suddenly realized that he was completely exhausted.

"I suppose you know what a darn fool stunt that was," Jason's father said grimly. "You nearly got yourselves killed out there."

Jason was half-lying on the sofa. He was wearing

some of Ricky's clothes, which were miles too big for him. And his ankle was wrapped in an Ace bandage and propped on a pillow. The doctor had said he'd be as good as new in a day or so. "Don't blame Ricky," he said. "He just came to rescue me."

"I blame both of you," his father replied. "Playing detective when you should have been thinking about more important things, such as school. If you really believed that you'd uncovered something serious, you should have gone to the proper authorities. And if you didn't believe that, you were simply wasting your time."

"Well, George," Martin Foster said, "no need to go to extremes here. Jason and Ricky did pass their information on to us as soon as they were reasonably sure of their facts. And while I certainly agree that they took an unnecessary risk this evening, I do think that if it hadn't been for their foresight, we might have had a problem on our hands."

"Ricky's foresight, you mean. From what I gather, my boy went off half-cocked and never mind the consequences."

"Be that as it may," Martin replied in a soothing voice, "a chemist from the Water Board has taken test samples from the stream and the reservoir. He's already concerned enough to get in touch with the mayor and Commissioner Dysan about the situation. It's just possible that your son has helped avert

a health crisis in Cascade."

Ricky was sitting on the floor in pajamas and a robe. The moment the boys arrived at the Foster home they'd taken showers and washed all over with brown soap, just as if they'd touched poison ivy. Ricky felt tired, but he was too excited to sleep.

"Then it really was Lake Fear," he said. "Do they know what the chemical is that's causing the trouble?"

"Probably not. The chemist said the tests may take two or three days."

Jason frowned. "What I don't understand is why the stream rose so fast. We wouldn't have been in any danger if it hadn't been for that."

"That's another mystery," Martin said. "Someone broke into the reservoir's control box and opened the floodgates, but it's not clear who or why. The sheriff told me his deputies caught someone leaving the area—a man named Thrippen. But whether he's connected to this or not, I don't know."

Thrippen? Ricky tried to think, but his mind seemed to be working very slowly. Where had he heard that name?

Then he had it. And with it came the key to the whole case. Thrippen was the orchard owner who had delivered the drums of pesticide to the crop-dusting plane. He knew Ricky had been asking the pilot about people dumping things in the lake! Somehow, some of the pesticides must have gotten into the water, causing the sickness. Maybe the incompetent pilot, the one Jules replaced, had dropped a load of the concentrated chemicals into the lake by mistake. By opening the floodgates, Thrippen must have hoped to destroy the evidence. It all fit together, and Ricky felt a surge of relief that the Institute's secret installation had no part in the solution.

"Dad?" he said. "I think I have the answer." He quickly explained about Thrippen and the crop dusting.

"Terrific, son! I don't suppose you also know what they were dusting the orchard with?" He smiled to show that he was teasing, but his face changed when Ricky told him the letters he had seen on the drums. "That stuff! I thought that had been banned years ago," he exclaimed. "I'd better get on the phone to the Water Board lab. This could shorten the testing a lot."

While Martin Foster went to telephone, Jason exchanged glances with Ricky. "Then Creep-o Kirk didn't have anything to do with it," he said. "I was hoping he was in trouble."

"Just another innocent victim—more or less," Ricky replied. With Jason's father in the room, it wasn't the time to discuss bootleg fireworks.

Jason gave a big yawn. "Well, partner, I guess we solved our case."

Ricky grinned. "I guess so, partner."

Martin reappeared. "The chemist was very excited by your information," he reported. "Apparently the kids' symptoms fit very closely with those of exposure to that pesticide. And I was right: it was banned in this country, though they still use it in Mexico and elsewhere. Thrippen knew that if anyone found out he was using it on his orchard, his whole crop would be destroyed."

"Why did he take a chance like that?" Jason asked.

"Simple greed, I suppose. I imagine that someone found a few dozen drums of it in a warehouse and offered them to him at a bargain price. And the stuff *is* very effective, though dangerous as well."

Jason's head was nodding. "It's time you boys were in bed," George Lindsay said gruffly. "Here, son, take my arm. I'll help you to the car. 'Night, Ricky; 'night, Martin. I'm grateful that it ended with no damage worse than a sore ankle."

Ricky's mother had spent the evening giving a lecture and slide show to the Audubon Society and had missed the uproar completely. When she got home, Martin started to fill her in. And Ricky took the opportunity to slip down to the basement and boot up the computer.

ALEC, THIS IS RICKY.

ABOUT TIME, TOO, ALEC grumped. I WAS STARTING

TO THINK YOU HAD DECIDED TO SPEND THE NIGHT IN THAT STREAM BED.

For a couple of moments Ricky was so happy to be in touch with ALEC again that he couldn't reply. Then he thought of an answer his friend would appreciate. THE MATTRESS WAS TOO LUMPY, he typed. WHERE HAVE YOU BEEN?

WERE YOU ALARMED? I APOLOGIZE. IT OCCURRED TO ME THAT OUR COMMUNICATION CHANNELS MIGHT BE UNDER CLOSE SCRUTINY. I SHUT DOWN TRANSMISSION UNTIL I WAS ABLE TO CHECK OUT THE POSSIBILITY THOROUGHLY. I IMAGINE YOU ARE AS EAGER AS I AM TO BE QUESTIONED BY FEDERAL AGENTS.

UNDER SCRUTINY BECAUSE OF THE SECRET FACILITY NEAR LAKE FEAR? Ricky asked.

I DON'T UNDERSTAND YOUR REFERENCE, ALEC replied blandly.

Ricky took the hint. The secret facility was a closed subject between them. BY THE WAY, he typed, WE FIGURED OUT THE ANSWER TO THE MYSTERY.

THRIPPEN AND THE PESTICIDE?

ALEC! YOU KNEW ALL ALONG! YOU'RE SHOWING OFF!

NO, AND NO. YOU TOLD ME ABOUT THE PESTICIDE THIS AFTERNOON. CORRELATING EFFECTS OF EXPOSURE WITH OUR SYMPTOMS TOOK ONLY A FEW NANOSECONDS. BUT I COULD NOT RISK GETTING THE INFORMATION TO YOU, AS I'VE EXPLAINED. I DO NOT BELIEVE IT WOULD HAVE HELPED MUCH AT THAT POINT, ANYWAY. AS FOR THRIPPEN, I

RETRIEVED HIS NAME FROM THE SHERIFF'S DEPART-
MENT'S ARREST RECORDS JUST BEFORE YOU SIGNED ON.

YOU KNEW WHEN I GOT IN TROUBLE, THOUGH.

I SURMISED IT. I KNEW THAT YOU WERE FOLLOWING A
TREACHEROUS PATH BESIDE A STREAM. WHEN THE COM-
PULATOR SHORTED OUT, IT SEEMED LIKELY THAT IT, AND
POSSIBLY YOU, HAD FALLEN IN. BUT I ONLY BEGAN TO
WORRY WHEN THE WATER BOARD COMPUTER REG-
ISTERED THE OPEN VALVES AT THE DAM.

Ricky's eyes narrowed. WERE YOU THE ONE WHO
SENT THE DEPUTIES WHO CAUGHT THRIPPEN?

NOT EXACTLY. I DID MAKE A FEW ADJUSTMENTS IN THE
ALARM PROGRAM INSTALLED ON THE WATER BOARD
CONTROLS. IT IS AN INEFFECTUAL SYSTEM, BUT IT SEEMS
TO HAVE FUNCTIONED VERY WELL THIS EVENING. SO FAR
THRIPPEN HAS JUST BEEN CHARGED WITH MALICIOUS
MISCHIEF. THEY MAKE OPENING THE FLOODGATES SOUND
LIKE A TRICK-OR-TREAT STUNT THAT WENT TOO FAR.

AND HE WAS GOING TO PASS OUT POISONED APPLES,
TOO, Ricky replied. ONE THING I WAS WONDERING
ABOUT: MY DAD COMPLIMENTED ME ON MY FORESIGHT.
WHAT WAS HE TALKING ABOUT?

OH. Even looking at letters on a screen, Ricky some-
how could tell that ALEC was embarrassed. YOUR
PERIL PLACED ME IN A DILEMMA, his friend continued. I
HAD TO ALERT SOMEONE TO RESCUE YOU, BUT I
PREFERRED NOT TO REVEAL MYSELF IN THE PROCESS.

Preferred not to . . ! Ricky knew how deeply his disembodied friend feared *any* degree of exposure. Yet ALEC had been willing to take that risk for Ricky's sake. Ricky had to blink several times and rub his eyes before he could focus on the screen.

FORTUNATELY IT WASN'T NECESSARY, ALEC continued. YOUR FATHER AND DR. STANLEY WERE LOGGED ON AT THE TIME. I SIMPLY BROKE IN WITH A MESSAGE FROM YOU, INDICATING YOUR LOCATION AND YOUR URGENT NEED OF ASSISTANCE.

HOW WAS I SUPPOSED TO HAVE SENT THIS MESSAGE?

DON'T YOU REMEMBER? ALEC teased. YOU FILED IT BEFORE YOU LEFT, WITH A PROGRAM THAT WOULD TRANSMIT IT AT A CERTAIN TIME UNLESS COUNTERMANDED. I THINK YOU SHOWED A LOT OF FORESIGHT, DON'T YOU?

NO, Ricky replied, I DON'T. BUT LUCKILY I HAVE A GOOD FRIEND TO GET ME OUT OF SCRAPES THAT I DON'T FORESEE.

THE ONLY DISADVANTAGE TO MY PLOY WAS THAT IT OCCASIONED A DELAY. I JUDGED THAT A MESSAGE TIMED FOR NINE O'CLOCK WOULD BE MORE CONVINCING THAN ONE PRESET FOR TRANSMISSION AT—SAY—8:51. I'M HAPPY THAT THE DELAY DID NO HARM.

Ricky was determined that, for once, he was going to have the last word. THAT'S RIGHT, he typed. BETTER LAKE THAN NEVER!

TWELVE

Ricky and Jason huddled under their umbrellas. The rain was falling so hard that drops bounced off the puddles. Why was the school bus always late on days like this, Ricky wondered.

Karen arrived, looking as bedraggled as her friends. "Hey," she called. "I hear you guys saved the whole town from being poisoned. Is that true?"

Two days had passed since the discovery of the pesticide dump. The investigation had proved Ricky's theory true, and all the papers had carried the story.

Ricky and Jason hadn't been mentioned by name, but obviously Karen had read between the lines.

All the kids at the bus stop stared at the boys, and Ricky felt his ears grow hot. But then the bus arrived, and everyone paid attention to climbing aboard.

"We'll tell you about it later," Ricky said as he slid into a seat across from Karen.

"Okay," she said, sensing his embarrassment. "As long as it's okay to drink the water." She glanced out the window. "There's enough of it coming down, that's for sure. Do you think after the hot spell all this rain will hurt the garden? I'd hate for our experiment to be ruined."

"Even if the garden's ruined, the experiment won't be," Ricky replied. "We're trying to find out how the fertilizers work under natural conditions. And what's more natural around here than rain?"

"Besides," Jason chimed in, "rain's good for plants—even if it isn't good for other things." He laughed and Ricky grinned broadly.

Karen frowned at them. "You guys have been up to something," she declared. "Aside from saving the town, I mean. You might as well tell me now, because I'm going to find out one way or another."

The two boys exchanged a glance. "Well," Ricky began, then stopped to see who was within listening distance. "You remember when Jerry Whiteside tried to sell us firecrackers?"

"Do I remember!" Karen's cheeks turned pink. "I reported him to the principal."

"You did?" Jason said. "That was gutsy."

"I had to. I kept thinking about some little kid being hurt when I could have prevented it."

"What happened when you told the principal?" Ricky asked.

Karen's face reddened even more. "He called Jerry in, and the creep denied it all. He said I was telling lies about him because I had a crush on him and he wasn't interested!"

"Nobody believed him, did they?"

"I hope not! Can you imagine anyone getting a crush on a drip like that? But it was my word against his, and I didn't have any evidence, so the principal said there was nothing he could do. I could have screamed! And I'm still worried about little kids getting hurt."

"I think you can stop worrying," Ricky said.

"Yeah," Jason added. "I don't think Jerry's fireworks are going to be much of a bang this year." He and Ricky exchanged grins.

"What do you mean?" Karen demanded. "Come on, you guys. Don't be so mysterious!"

"Well," Jason said, "Ricky found out where Jerry and his buddies were hiding their fireworks supply. The only problem was, they found Ricky about the time he found the dump. He got away and they decided to find another place to stash the goods."

"They had a lot of stuff, though," Ricky said, "and with all the activity up near Lake Farnsworth, we figured that they wouldn't be able to shift the crates very far. So yesterday evening we went up there, and hunted around until we found the new hiding place."

"That's wonderful," Karen exclaimed. "Did you call the police?"

"Nooo . . ." said Jason. "There was a small problem. If we told the police where the stuff was, Kirk and his gang would know right away that Ricky was to blame, and they'd come after him. Now Ricky isn't scared, of course—"

"My knees always shake this way," Ricky said.

"—but why ask for unnecessary trouble?"

"You just left all those terrible fireworks sitting there?" Karen demanded. "I can't believe it!"

"That's just what we did," Jason replied cheerfully. "But I have a funny feeling that when the guys go up there today, they'll find that the tarp blew off of their merchandise. With all this rain, it wouldn't surprise me if those beautiful fireworks got ruined."

Ricky's grin grew wider. "I wonder which of them will get the blame for the knot that came undone? Maybe they'll all blame each other and start quarreling. That'd really be great!"

"Or maybe they'll blame Lake Fear," said Jason.

"By now everyone knows it's bad luck."

"Bad luck for bad guys," Ricky said. "Without them hanging around, it may be a pretty friendly place."

"Maybe you should give it a new nickname," suggested Karen. "Call it Lake Friendly from now on."

"I don't think I could stomach that," said Ricky.

"Yeah. Let's not do anything rash," said Jason.

And to Karen's complete mystification, they burst into laughter.